D1388201

SLUGS

It was almost three a.m. when he came round. His head was thumping from the combined effect of the fall and the whisky.

Ron felt something wet on his chin and, for a second, thought he'd vomited but then he felt something fat and slimy gliding over his lips and into his open mouth. He snapped his teeth together, biting down on the jellied lump, cutting it in half. A foul, obscene taste filled his mouth and, as he tried to scream, half of the sticky lump rolled back into his throat. Ron coughed, feeling the hot bile clawing its way up from his stomach. He put a hand up to his cut and, as his probing fingers found the gash in his scalp, he felt a plump, mucus-covered form burrowing into the wound itself...

Slugs

SHAUN HUTSON

AUTHOR'S NOTE

If I lived to be one hundred, wrote five books a year and won the Booker Prize every year (yes I am joking) there is just one book I'd probably be remembered for and it's SLUGS. And I'm very grateful for that. It launched me, it made my name (I'm not quite sure as what) and it's stuck with me throughout what has remained of my career.

The fact that it was filmed (not particularly well I hasten to add) doubtless helped and certainly the anecdotes surrounding the book and the film have given me something to talk about since it was first published back in 1982.

I never wanted to do a book about flesh eating slugs, originally the book was to be about blood sucking leeches which were radioactive and would transform their victims into vampires (elements of the story would later be integrated into EREBUS two years later) but I had written a novel called DEATHDAY which had been published in the U.S the previous year under the name of Robert Neville that featured a scene with a giant slug and my agent at the time said "why not write a book all about slugs?"

As I was only 23 at the time this seemed like a really dumb idea. How the fuck would slugs kill and eat people? It wasn't as if they could outrun them was it? However, as this agent (Bob Tanner) was also the man who had published James Herbert's "THE RATS" I was reasonably sure he knew what he was talking about when it came to terror by animals books so, I went off and did some research and discovered enough about slugs to realize that there was more than enough material for a novel. Not only were there three species of carnivorous slug in this country, they could also spread a disease that caused worms to grow in victims brains. I was in heaven! The book was like a throw-back to the "terror by animals" films of the fifties when radioactive creatures ranging from giant squids to huge lizards attacked mankind. The thing with SLUGS was that these creatures were only six inches long and they weren't radioactive or demonic. They actually existed.

As was my way in those days the book was written quickly (less than three months as I remember) and had only minimal editing (I know some will say that's obvious!). It was launched with a huge splurge of publicity that included bus front advertising and radio advertising and it actually became a best-seller. I was delighted and amazed and went into shock when I got the first royalty statement! I was also inundated with letters from people telling me how good the book was and how much they hated slugs. It seemed I'd touched a nerve. Even before the book was written I'd been told that five years later I'd do a sequel (which duly appeared in the shape of BREEDING GROUND in 1986) and then five years after that I'd do a third instalment which never materialized due to various circumstances.

Not long after its release a Spanish company acquired the film rights to SLUGS and the film appeared a few years later. I first saw it on a big screen at a Horror Film Festival in London. The organisers had flown a copy from the States specially to show at the festival and asked me to attend. Fuck me, talk about embarrassing. Obviously every author wants their work to be faithfully brought to the screen but it's a lottery to be honest. I just wish they'd paid more money for the rights to make the transition less painful!

It's weird but over the years it's achieved this kind of cult status that only truly bad films can acquire but, having said that, I've sat through much worse films over the years and if you put SLUGS up against any of the TWILIGHT movies or any number of so called "popular" films since 1988 I'd watch SLUGS anytime.

But, back to the book. It was very successful and spawned an entire sub-genre of "terror by animals" books such as BLOWFLY, EAT THEM ALIVE (about giant preying mantises), CARACAL, BATS, COMES A SPIDER etc. etc. In fact, the only thing that no one wrote about was leeches! Perhaps I should do that some day.

I still shudder when I see slugs in the garden, they are truly revolting things to look at I think but the weird thing was, until SLUGS was published I had never seen any of them around the house but on the day the book was published I went to get the milk in from the front step and there were two on the bottles! Maybe they knew something I didn't...

Shaun Hutson 2016

This book is dedicated to my daughter, Kelly and not just because she missed it the first time around.

Acknowledgements

Thank you to the following people for reasons which they will appreciate. Meg Davis, Darren Laws and Holly Andrews at Caffeine Nights, Graeme Sayer, Rod Smallwood and Phantom Music. Steve, Bruce, Dave, Nicko, Janick and Adrian. My Mum, obviously. All the management and staff at Cineworld Milton Keynes especially Mark, Dani, Adam, Phillip, Alun, Mel, Hannah, James, Rae, Phil and anyone else I've forgotten. A big thanks also to the Broadway Cinema in Letchworth. A huge thank you to all of my readers who bought this book the first time around and, of course, to all of you who've bought it since.

'The Devil Damn thee Black ...'

- Macbeth; Act V; Scene 111

PROLOGUE

The slug's eye stalks waved slowly as it moved towards the crimson lump on which several of its companions were already feeding. It slithered onto the meat and buried the long central tooth in the flesh, its rows of sharp radular teeth moving back and forth like rasps as it chewed off pieces of meat, enjoying the new coppery taste of blood.

The slugs had grown accustomed to this taste over the past few months, hidden away in the cellar beneath the old house, they had discovered this new source of food. They had tired of their hunting and concentrated, instead, on the raw meat which was tossed down into the rank, fetid darkness. A dozen or so swarmed over the rotted chop, covering it with their own slime trails, chewing until there was nothing but a tiny bone left.

At one time, the slugs had been forced to compete with the other scavengers in the cellar for the precious scraps. With the cockroaches, the wood-lice and centipedes. But now, with a regular supply of meat, they were the dominant group. By sheer weight of numbers, they had made the damp cellar their own. When there were no scraps they fed on the other creatures which shared their pitch black domain. Sometimes they fed on each other.

They had begun to breed more prolifically and many had increased in size. Even though the cellar was large, its floor was covered by them, a vast seething black mass almost invisible in the impenetrable gloom. Only a single shaft of weak light broke through the darkness, forcing its way in by way of a small hole in the cellar bulkhead. But, the slugs paid it no heed. They enjoyed the blackness and the damp and they waited eagerly for the bloodied scraps.

They had heard the footsteps above them many times, felt the vibrations. It made them restless.

In that stinking cellar they slithered over one another in their impatience like an undulating black carpet.

The footsteps seemed to grow louder each day.

One

Ron Bell got through one verse of 'Mull of Kintyre' then threw up. He slumped heavily against the wooden gatepost, wondering why the world was spinning round so fast. He bent double over the fence, clutching his stomach, trying to persuade the remaining Scotch to retreat back down his gullet. He swallowed hard and blew out his cheeks. A thin film of perspiration had formed on his face and he muttered to himself as his stomach continued to somersault. He turned and gazed up at the street lamp, its sodium glare reminding him of a gigantic glow worm. Amused at his little analogy, Ron started to giggle. He pushed open the gate and stumbled down the path towards. the front of the house, stumbling once over one of the chipped granite slabs. He fell forward, the bottle of Haig dropping from his grasp. It landed in the thick grass on one side of the path and remained unbroken. Ron felt something wet beneath him as he sat up and he thought it was the whisky. He put a hand to the crutch of his trousers and started to giggle again.

'Please let it be blood,' he said, laughing loudly. The sound carried far in the stillness of the night and someone walking past the gate peered at him disdainfully.

'Evening,' Ron slurred, trying to get up. He spotted the Haig bottle lying in the waist high grass and retrieved it gratefully, realising at the same time that he'd wet himself. A dark stain was fanning out from his crutch, staining one leg of his trousers too.

'Shit,' he murmured and stumbled on towards the front door. He spotted some ants hurrying away from his clumsy feet and wagged a reproachful finger at them.

'Isn't it about time you lot were in bed?' he chuckled. 'Dirty stop-outs.' With a gleeful whoop, he brought his foot down on the nearest group of insects, crushing them into the pavement. Laughing like an idiot, he made his way up the remainder of the path, rummaging through his pockets for the front door key. He stuffed the whisky bottle into his coat pocket and steadied himself for the difficult task of trying to find the key hole. At the third attempt he made it and tumbled into the hall, his nostrils immediately assailed by the familiar odour of damp. But it was a smell he'd come to live with, almost to welcome. He slapped on the hall light and, being careful to remove the Haig bottle first, slung his coat at the rack. It missed and landed in an untidy heap. Ron looked at it for a moment then blundered into the sitting room. He flicked the light switch. The bulb glowed brilliantly for a second then, with a loud pop, blew out.

'Shit,' grunted Ron. To hell with it, he'd manage without. At half past eleven at night, pissed out of his mind he didn't fancy clambering up step ladders to put a new bulb in. He staggered across the room towards the small portable TV set up on the sideboard. He yelped in pain as he banged his shin on the coffee table and he bent to rub the injured spot, cursing to himself. He finally groped his way to the TV and pressed the ON button, watching as a hazy monochrome picture gradually took shape. Ron fiddled with the aerial until the people on screen possessed the regulation number of heads then he fumbled in the cabinet beneath for a glass. All he could find was a pint pot. He shrugged and, clutching the tankard, stumbled back towards his chair. He bumped his shin again and, as he bent to massage the throbbing bruise, he caught sight of his own reflection in the glass top of the table. His eyes were sunken into their sockets and it looked as if someone had coloured his lower lids with charcoal. The accumulated growth of four days whiskers licked around his chin and cheeks and crackled as he ran a rough hand across them. He shook his head and reached his chair, slumping into the threadbare seat. A spring dug him hard in the backside and he jumped, almost dropping his tankard. Muttering to himself, he unscrewed the cap on the whisky bottle and half filled the pint pot, watching the bubbles rise to the top of the amber liquid. He swallowed the fiery fluid in deep gulps, gasping when he'd finished. He sat for long moments, gazing at the flickering TV screen, not seeing what was on. His mind was elsewhere. He rubbed his bruised shin once more and looked at the coffee table angrily.

Bloody monstrosity. Margaret had bought it not long after they moved into the house. She said it gave the house a touch of class. Ron scoffed at the recollection. What the hell had she known about class? He smiled, wondering what she would have thought seeing him the way he was now. It had been more than two years since she'd walked out on him. It was as if, all his life, he'd been living a false existence, trying to be something he really wasn't. He'd been manager at the local branch of Sainsbury's and it was his salary which had enabled them to buy the house in the first place. The last owner had left it in pretty good nick and there was no need for full scale renovation. A fact which pleased Ron no end, never having been one for painting and decorating. The house was old but without the feeling of antiquity usually felt in buildings erected at the turn of the century. In the beginning they had lived happily together, had built a nice home but Ron had just got bored. As simple as that. He started off by having an affair with one of the cashiers in the supermarket. He usually worked late hours so Margaret never suspected but his ruin had come with the arrival of Debbie. She had been seventeen the first time Ron went to bed with her and, at forty-two, he'd had trouble keeping up with her. By God, she knew what was what between the sheets, he remembered wistfully. He was smitten. He bought her gifts, he took her out, no longer seeming to care whether Margaret found out or not. The money dwindled. Bills didn't get paid.

Then, one weekend, Margaret had gone to stay with her sister and Ron had invited Debbie to stay. He'd never forgotten that weekend. They spent nearly all their time in bed and she was insatiable. So caught up in their wanton lovemaking was he, Ron didn't even notice Margaret standing in the bedroom doorway watching them. She'd come back a day early.

He didn't even try to explain.

Margaret packed her bags that night and walked out on him.

Debbie had tired of him two weeks later and finished the affair. She'd had his money and his love but she only wanted the former. So, for the past two years he'd lived alone in the old house, watching it go to seed as he did himself. His work suffered. He received endless reprimands from his superiors until, finally, after over-ordering the wrong product three weeks running, he'd been dismissed.

After that it was onto the dole. The bills piled up, the rates were overdue and, just that morning, the eviction notice had arrived. He reached for it, picking it up from the table beside him and waving the manila envelope before him. Inside, an official notice told him that he had twenty-four hours to come up with the money or he'd be forcibly evicted. Fuck them, thought Ron, they'll have to drag me out of here bodily. He emptied the bottle of Haig into the pint pot and tossed the empty receptacle over his shoulder where it shattered against the wall. His head felt as if someone had wrapped a blanket around it. The images on the TV blurred and Ron grunted as he downed the last of the Scotch. They were playing 'God Save the Queen' on the telly and, swaying precariously, Ron stood up and saluted until the music died away. The announcer reminded him to switch his set off and the screen dissolved into a network of lines and dots, the hiss of static making it sound like an enraged snake. Ron put a hand to his head then stepped forward to turn the set off.

Once more he banged into the coffee table but, this time, he overbalanced. Arms flailing like a human windmill, he toppled over the table and crashed heavily to the ground, catching his head on the corner of the sideboard as he fell. He felt a sharp pain as his scalp seemed to split and he went down in a heap before the hissing TV. Blood began to pump freely from the ragged cut and Ron raised one hand as if in silent reproach. Then, with a final groan, he blacked out.

It was almost three a.m. when he came round. His head was thumping from the combined effect of the fall and the whisky and, above him, the TV continued to hiss and crackle. The cut on his head must have been worse than he thought because it seemed to be throbbing mightily. His hair was matted with blood and some of it had run down over his eyes, crusting on the -lids and making it difficult to see.

He felt something wet on his chin and, for a second, thought he'd vomited but then he felt something fat and slimy gliding over his lips and into his open mouth. Ron snapped his teeth together, biting down on the jellied lump, cutting it in half. A foul, obscene taste filled his mouth and, as he tried to scream, half of the sticky lump rolled back into his throat. Ron coughed, feeling the hot bile clawing its way up from his stomach. He put a hand up to his cut and, as his probing fingers found the gash in his scalp, he felt a plump, mucus-covered form burrowing into the wound itself. Ron shrieked and tugged at the pulsating shape, finally pulling it free.

For long seconds he held the slug before him, his eyes bulging wide with terror, his own blood covering the head of the foul creature. Then, with a despairing moan, he hurled the monstrosity across the room. But, it was as he did so that he became aware of the pain which was gnawing at his legs and his other arm. Scarcely able to comprehend the sight before him, he saw that his limbs were covered by a seething black mass of these creatures, all slipping and sliding over one another in their efforts to get at his warm flesh. They were on his stomach too, burrowing into the skin and muscle. With a mixture of terror and disbelief, he realised that they were eating him.

He tried to crawl, dragging the monstrous parasites with him. But his hands pressed down onto a jellied carpet of slugs which seemed to be rising from the very floor itself. He fell onto his face and one of the revolting beasts slid into his mouth, fastening its razor-sharp central tooth into his tongue. He felt the bile rising once more, mingling with the taste of his own blood and the sickening mucus of the fat slug. The beast slipped down his gullet and fastened itself into the lining of his throat. Blood began to fill his mouth, spilling out onto the other slugs which were rapidly engulfing him. He felt as though his head was swelling. He couldn't breathe and even the sharp hissing of the TV seemed to have stopped. One of the slugs was burrowing into his ear, seeking out the juicy grey meat of the brain. Ron's body began to shake uncontrollably as the slugs finally swarmed over him, digging deep into his muscles, enjoying the taste of the blood which gushed so violently from his body.

One of them bored into his jugular vein and a great fountain of crimson erupted from the torn blood vessel. It splattered up the wall as if sprayed from a hose pipe.

The slugs stripped the body clean of flesh then they devoured the softer internal organs. Their eye stalks waved about as they slithered over the corpse, their mouths moving constantly, tasting the warm blood. It had formed a pool around the body, soaking into the rotted floorboards, mingling with the mucoid slime which the creatures themselves had left behind. And then, when there was nothing left worth eating, they retreated back slowly to the cellar, to the darkness.

The remains of Ron Bell lay in the centre of the room, one uneaten eyeball bulging madly in the riven socket.

Below, the slugs slithered about. There were many who had not yet eaten and they were restless, as if sensing that this was just the beginning.

Two

The alarm clock went off dead on seven, its strident ringing filling the room. Mike Brady shot out a hand to silence the clock but only succeeded in knocking it off the bedside table. Still ringing, it fell to the carpet and skidded away from his groping hand. He forced his sleep encrusted eyes open and saw that the damn thing was lying about a foot away, just out of reach.

'Oh, sod it,' he groaned, gazing at the clock as if willing it to be silent. Another few seconds ringing and he scrambled out of bed, snatched up the bloody thing and depressed the button on the top. He sat on the edge of the bed eyeing the clock malevolently. The warm shape in bed beside him didn't stir. Brady looked down at her sleeping form and smiled, then he leant over and gently bit her exposed shoulder. She awoke with a start and rolled over, looking up into Brady's smiling face. He held up the clock and tapped the perspex cover indicating the time.

'Rise and shine,' said Brady, slipping a hand under the covers. He tickled her stomach and she started to laugh, although it sounded like an effort. Kim Brady rolled onto her side and gently prodded her husband's belly.

'Fatso,' she said, tugging at a roll of fat with her thumb and forefinger.

Brady looked indignant and got to his feet, crossing to the full length mirror which covered the wardrobe door. He stood before it and drew in his stomach, holding his breath. Defiantly he turned to face her.

'Fatso my arse,' he said but then he lost control and his stomach flopped forward again. They both laughed.

'It comes with your age,' she said, smiling, watching as Brady got down on all fours and began a series of jerky press-ups.

'Look, it's bad enough being forty without having you remind me all the time,' he wheezed, his face turning the colour of over-ripe tomatoes. He finally got to his feet. 'Oh to hell with it. You'll just have to like me fat.'

'I'm only kidding, Mike,' she said, smiling, motioning for him to come back to bed. He sat down beside her, his eyes momentarily straying to her firm breasts, rising and falling gently as she breathed. At thirty-five, Kim Brady still had a figure to be proud of. She blinked myopically at her husband and reached for her glasses, which were on the table beside her, propped up on two Erica Jong novels. But Brady stopped her, instead drawing her close, his mouth pressing urgently against hers, each tongue seeking the warmth of the other. He ran his hand gently across her face then kissed her softly on the forehead. She fumbled for her glasses and pushed them on.

'And stop going on about being forty,' she chided. 'It's not for another month yet and besides,' she started to giggle, 'life…'

He interrupted her. '…begins at forty. Yes I know, that's what everybody keeps telling me.'

'You know, I was thinking,' she said, the mischievous grin still on her face. 'Being married to a man five years older than me does have its advantages.'

He raised his eyebrows quizzically.

'It means we can both start drawing our pension at the same time.'

He nodded affably.

'It's after seven you know,' he told her. 'Isn't it time *you* got up?' He rose and crossed to the wardrobe, taking out a shirt and tie, hanging them on the handle while he took out his familiar two-piece grey suit.

'I'm not going in today,' she told him. 'The nursery's closed for a couple of days.'

He looked round. 'Why?'

'Industrial action by the tea ladies or something,' she said.

Brady grunted. 'I don't blame them, the lousy bloody wages they pay them.' He sighed. 'I know one thing. I wish to Christ I didn't have to go in today.' He walked into the adjoining bathroom and Kim heard the sound of his electric razor humming.

'Why not?' she called. 'I thought you liked your job.'

'There's nothing wrong with the job,' he called back, flicking the razor off and running some hot water into the sink. 'It's just that I don't fancy what they've got lined up for me today.'

Kim sat in silence, listening as he washed his face then she heard the hiss and splutter of the shower and, a second later, a pair of pyjama trousers came flying into the bedroom. She smiled. After a moment or two, the shower was turned off and Brady re-emerged into the bedroom, a towel wrapped around his waist. He rubbed himself down and started to dress.

'They're serving an eviction notice on Ron Bell,' he told her. 'You know, the bloke who lives in that old house just outside the town centre.'

'The one near the new estate?' she asked.

He nodded. 'He's about six months behind with the rates and there have been complaints from the residents of the estate about him and the house. The garden's like a bloody jungle. I dread to think what the inside of the place looks like.'

'But I don't understand why you've got to go along,' she said, looking puzzled.

'I've got to drive the bailiff to the house,' he explained. 'They can already sling the poor sod out for non -payment of rates and because of the complaints against him but that's not enough for our council,' he said acidly. 'They want me to write a report on the state of the building, how disgusting it is and how Ron Bell isn't fit to keep it tidy. He's already hung and drawn, they've left the quartering to me'. He pulled his tie tight, smoothing it out and inspecting his image in the mirror. Brady exhaled deeply and pulled on his jacket. He gazed at his own reflection for long moments. Mike Brady, Council Health Inspector. He smiled to himself. He'd held that exalted position for the last fourteen years, two years longer than he'd been married to Kim. Coincidentally, they'd first met at the offices. She'd been a secretary, he'd just arrived from London where he'd been doing the same job. Some of the jobs he'd had in Merton had been child's play after the revelations in London. He'd seen some things there which had made his hair curl. If he had a pound for every hamburger and hot dog seller he'd forced off the streets during those early days he wouldn't need to work, he told himself. Flies on the meat, sausages made out of boiled down pigs' heads, hamburgers with every known type of bacteria alive infesting them, fat two inches deep in the serving trays. Some of the restaurants hadn't been much better. He still remembered the time he'd nearly eaten a curry which was later found to contain mouse droppings, or the incident when he'd walked into one kitchen to see the chef removing maggots from a side of beef he was about to put into the oven.

But, things in Merton were quieter. Even so he'd had his fair share of incidents. Like the house where-the ceiling had caved in because the kids had wet the bed so many times and the floorboards had rotted. Twelve of them in that family he remembered, most of the ten kids slept in one bed and they had about three pairs of shoes between them. Other than that, there hadn't been too much to bother him, just the usual drizzle of complaints. Blocked drains, the occasional cockroach infestation, the odd shady snack bar but the thing which Brady liked most about his job was that he had no one breathing down his neck all the time. He could get on with things in his own way, as long as the reports were in on time he never even saw any members of the council. This fact suited him admirably, he had nothing to thank them for, there was no love lost between the Conservative council and their Public Health Officer who was fond of voicing his socialist views loudly and often. The only good thing, as far as Brady was concerned was that his job had enabled him to meet Kim. They'd been immediately attracted to one another and had married in less than a year of meeting. The only thing which hurt him, and it hurt more because he knew the heartbreak it caused Kim, was that they were childless and always would be.

Three years after they had married she had been involved in a car accident. Five months pregnant at the time she'd lost the baby and also, due to the severe internal damage she sustained, had been told that she would never be able to bear children. The shock had been overwhelming, hitting them both much harder than he could have imagined. Kim in particular went through a seemingly endless period of depression during which Brady began to fear for her sanity but she got through it in the end and the experience seemed to strengthen their marriage, intensifying their love beyond imagination. For the last six years she had worked in the local nursery, her own thwarted maternal instincts now lavished upon the children of others.

When Brady turned away from the mirror, Kim was getting out of bed. He watched her slip on a paint-stained blouse (the one which she'd worn when they had decorated the place after first moving in) and a pair of faded denims, having to pull just a bit too hard to get them up over her hips. She finally managed it and fastened the button, puffing slightly. He smiled as he watched her and she looked up to see him grinning at her.

'Looks like I'm not the only one who needs to lose some weight,' he said, nodding towards her.

She picked up one of her slippers and threw it at him.

'Cheeky bugger,' she said. 'I've a good mind to make you get your own breakfast.'

He slapped her across the backside and they both made their way downstairs.

Three

Brady wound down the window of the Vauxhall Victor and allowed some of the crisp morning air to blow into the car. It was less than ten minutes' drive from their house to the council offices where he was to pick up Archie Reece, the bailiff, and take him to Ron Bell's house to serve the eviction notice. Brady really wasn't relishing the trip. He'd only met Reece a couple of times but there was something about the man that he didn't like. He seemed to enjoy his job. Evicting people from their homes was more like a hobby for him. Brady remembered the last time it had happened. The house owner had decided that he didn't want to be moved and Reece had promptly whacked him over the head with a chair leg in full view of the poor sod's horrified family. The unfortunate man had spent two months in hospital after that particular brush with Reece. However, the Health Inspector somehow didn't see Ron Bell as the type to put up much of a fight.

He drove at a leisurely pace, taking in the long rows of trees which lined the roadside, already heavy with blossom they brought a sweet odour wafting into the car which Brady sucked in gratefully. Even though it was early, the sun had risen high in the sky and it promised to be a scorcher. The blossom seemed to catch the rays of the sun, holding it until it glowed pink and white like flimsy neon clusters.

A sixteen wheeler drove past in the opposite direction and Brady coughed as a choking cloud of diesel fumes swept into the car. He waved a hand in front of his face and glanced into the rear view mirror, watching the huge lorry swing up to the left, heading for the industrial part of town.

Despite its size, Merton had a prosperous industrial estate, comprising a foundry, a factory which made dust-carts and, the dominant business, a huge computer complex which manufactured the machines for places all around the globe. There was also a sizeable chemical works. The town had suffered its share of closures and redundancies as had all the other towns in the area, but, on the whole, the community was thriving.

Brady swung the Vauxhall into the car park of the council offices, glancing up at the clock above the building. The metal hands had reached eight thirty and the Health Officer checked his watch. He retrieved his briefcase from the back seat, locked his door and headed towards the flight of broad stone steps which led up to the main doors of the council offices. The building itself was a large, brownstone edifice built over a hundred years ago, and a century of accumulated muck was being removed by a posse of workmen who were at this moment swarming over the lower storeys of the building like so many boiler-suited ants repairing a break in the nest wall. Brady nodded affably to the foreman as he passed. The man was sitting cross-legged on the lowest walkway of the scaffolding, drinking coffee from a thermos flask.

The Health Inspector pushed open the double doors and walked in.

Brief greetings were exchanged with the two women on the reception deck and then Brady took the stairs to the second floor where his office lay.

He found Archie Reece waiting for him outside the office door.

The bailiff tried to smile but it came out as a leer and Brady just nodded in return and walked past him into his office. The other man followed him in and stood impatiently at the door watching as Brady crossed to his desk and sat down. There were three letters lying there and Reece exhaled noisily and irritably when he saw the Health Inspector open the first of them.

The bailiff held up a brown envelope.

'The eviction order on Ron Bell,' he said.

'I know,' said Brady, opening the second letter.

'You're supposed to drive me there, Mr Brady.'

The Health Inspector looked at Reece with distaste. He was a big man, broad and very muscular even though the folds of his ill-fitting suit did their best to conceal that fact. Brady guessed his height to be around six two and his hair, although white, was thick and flowing, almost covering his collar. His hands looked huge, big enough to encircle Brady's head with little effort. He was tapping agitatedly against the door frame with his stubby fingers.

'Is there a bloody deadline on it?' asked Brady.

Reece nodded. 'I'm supposed to have him out by nine.' He looked at his watch. 'It's quarter to, now.' He turned his gaze back to the Health Inspector who rose to his feet, fumbling in his jacket pocket for his car keys.

'Come on, then,' he said, irritably.

'I'm only doing my job,' Reece protested, following the younger man out of the office towards the stairs. They descended hurriedly and Brady led him out to the waiting Vauxhall. Reece slumped heavily into the passenger seat and rummaged around in his pocket, finally producing a packet of Rothmans.

'Don't smoke in here please,' said Brady, looking at him disdainfully. 'If *you* want to die of lung cancer that's your business. I bank on being around a bit longer.' He twisted the key in the ignition, stuck the car into first and pulled out.

Reece took the cigarette from his mouth and pushed it carefully back into the packet. He found a packet of mints in his other pocket.

'Is it all right if I have one of these?' he asked, defiantly. 'Or are you frightened of catching diabetes too?'

Brady looked at the big man as he pushed the mint into his mouth.

'Do you know what they use as sweeteners in those?' he asked, a slight smile on his lips.

Reece shook his head, gazing out of the front window.

'Recycled pig swill,' Brady told him, laughing aloud as the bailiff coughed and spat the mint out of the open window.

In five minutes they had reached Ron Bell's house.

Reece was out of the car with a speed implying relish and Brady could see the slight hint of a smile on the big man's lips. The Health Inspector locked the car and followed the bailiff, who, by this time, was through the gate and heading up the path to the front door of the house. Brady walked more slowly, his eyes moving slowly over the building and the garden. Jesus, he thought, talk about run-down. The grass on either side of the cracked path brushed against him as he walked and he lengthened his stride to avoid the scurrying ants which were oozing up from the crack in the granite like soil. The windows reflected the sun back at the two men, and that combined with the filth on them, made it impossible to see inside. Reece knocked three times on the front door and waited for an answer. Brady wandered across to the nearest window. It had wooden shutters on it, the wood itself rotted and yellowed in places. One was hanging off the hinges. He put his face to the pane and squinted into the gloom, trying to make out some sign of movement in what he took to be the dining room.

Reece banged the door again, harder this time.

'Perhaps he's out,' said Brady, wearily, sauntering back to the door.

Reece ignored the remark and repeated his frenzied attack on the door, as if willing it to open by itself. Brady shook his head.

'Bell,' shouted Reece, looking up at the windows of the first floor.

'For Christ's sake,' said the Health Inspector.

'I'm going to break in,' Reece told him. The bailiff strode off down the path to the window where Brady had just been. He took off his jacket, wrapped it around his elbow and, with one powerful backward stroke, broke the glass. Lumps of dirty crystal fell into the room and landed on the bare floor. Reece reached through and opened the window, hoisting himself over the sill. He landed on the broken glass which crunched beneath his heavy shoes. Brady followed him, the sound of the crushed glass reminding him of walking in heavy frost. Both men were immediately assailed by the smell of damp and Reece coughed, waving a hand in front of him. Dust particles floated lazily in the rays of sunlight which cut through the gloom.

'Bell,' Reece called again but only silence greeted his shout. He pointed to a door at the far end of the room and the two men headed towards it.

It was Brady who heard the sound first.

'Listen,' he said, lowering his voice for reasons even he didn't understand.

Reece stopped impatiently and cocked an ear in the direction of the sound. It was a high pitched, unceasing, hum which grew louder as they approached the door. The big man looked at Brady and shrugged. The handle to the door was rusty and pieces of brown metal peeled off like scabrous flesh as the bailiff turned it. It swung open with a loud creak and both men walked into the sitting room.

The stench which met them was almost palpable and even Brady recoiled at its ferocity. He just had time to register that the high pitched hum was coming from the TV which was still on, then his attention turned to the thing in the centre of the room.

Reece too saw it and Brady was vaguely aware of the big man sagging against the door frame, clutching his stomach.

'Jesus Christ,' he groaned, trying to retain his breakfast.

Brady took a step closer, the realization slowly spreading through him. The shapeless mass of torn flesh and shining bone which occupied the centre of the room was all that remained of Ron Bell. The Health Inspector moved closer, as close as the choking odour would allow him. The room was like a charnel house. Congealed blood was splattered up the walls and around the body, its rusty colour matching that of the old door handle. One sightless eye fixed Brady in a baleful stare. He pulled out his handkerchief and pressed it to his face but the foul stench even seemed to penetrate the material.

The corpse still retained some shreds of flesh, covering the shiny bones like wisps of gossamer, and clumps of hair still clung defiantly to what was left of the head. The mouth was open, revealing many rotted teeth, the lower jaw having been eaten through. It yawned soundlessly, the ligaments and tendons which had held it in place were gone. Part of the nose remained, the solitary nostril choked with clotted blood.

Reece seemed to have recovered his wits a little and he looked over at Brady, who was still kneeling beside the mutilated body.

'What the fucking hell happened to him?' gasped the bailiff, his breath coming in short gasps.

Brady didn't answer, he had finally managed to tear his gaze away from the body long enough to study the bare floorboards around it. They felt spongy because of the congealed blood which had soaked into the wood but it wasn't that which attracted the Health Inspector's eye. It was the shiny substance which seemed to cover the floor, sparkling like oil on water when the sun catches it. He noticed that it was all over the corpse too.

'How long's he been dead?' asked Reece, wiping a thin film of perspiration from his face.

Brady shrugged. 'It's hard to say. From the appearance of the body I'd say he'd been dead for months but...' He allowed the sentence to trail off. He stood up. 'You'd better phone the police.'

Reece nodded, happy to be able to escape the reeking confines of this slaughterhouse. Brady heard him exit then he leant back against the door frame, his eyes sweeping around the room.

There was more of the shiny substance on the far wall, only there it seemed to break apart into small trails each about an inch wide. He stroked his chin thoughtfully and looked down. There was more of the stuff at his feet. He knelt and felt tempted to touch it, much as a child does with something that arouses its curiosity but, at the last minute, he withdrew his hand, reaching instead to the inside pocket of his jacket. He took out a pencil and poked the end into the shiny stuff, seeing that it was fluid, but thick and sticky and, when he removed the pencil, the mucoid slime stuck to it. Brady wrinkled his forehead and laid the pencil down on the nearby sideboard.

He took one last look around the room and hurried out to see where Reece had got to.

The high pitched hum of the TV continued.

Four

Night brought with it a cloying humidity which made sleep, for many people, difficult. There was no moon and just the sodium glare of the street lamps penetrated the darkness.

Some of the houses on the new estate overlooked Ron Bell's house and some of those tenants had watched that afternoon as first the police and then an ambulance had arrived at the old place, but few had taken much notice. Perhaps the bloke had been taken ill, a heart attack perhaps. No one knew. No one cared. Some were pleased that he was gone, perhaps now the house would be sold to someone who would look after it and preferably to someone who would get that maze of a garden into some semblance of order. But, the subject of Ron Bell and his house was only of passing interest to the inhabitants of the new estate. Now, with night well and truly upon them, they tried to sleep in their little houses which had become like ovens due to the weather.

In dozens of red brick dwellings, they dozed, snored, made love, watched television or sat and talked. Crying children were attended to, pets dozed in the heat and, somewhere on the estate, a couple of tom-cats fought out their nightly duel. They hissed and spat at one another, scratching and biting in one of the gardens until a well-aimed ash-tray, thrown from one of the bedroom windows, put an end to their squabble.

Silence descended once more.

In the cellar of Ron Bell's house it was silent too, except for the slurping, sucking sounds the slugs made as they slithered over one another. There seemed to be so many of them now. The cellar was filled practically to overflowing and, besides, their source of food had disappeared. Their hunger became uncontrollable and they began to slither up towards the hole in the bulkhead, towards the night air. Some burrowed through the ground, others slithered through the waist high grass which parted as if moved by some invisible hand. Their jet black colour helped them blend into the night.

But most crawled to the sewer cover which lay in the garden. Rusty and covered in moss, it was surrounded by broken concrete and the slugs found many holes. They crawled down into the black depths, welcoming the wetness which enabled them to move faster. Many even slipped into the filthy water, carried along by its flow.

Through the earth, over it and swept along by the fast flowing sewers, they moved towards the new estate, an invisible unstoppable black horde.

Five

Mary Forbes watched as her two children disappeared around the bend in the road, waving to them one last time before she retreated back inside the house. She smiled happily to herself as she crossed to the windows in the front room. She unfastened them and pushed them open, allowing the slight breeze to blow in. It brought with it the heady scent of lavender and Mary looked out into the garden with pride at the blossoming purple flowers. The DJ on the radio told her it was eight fifty-one and then his exaggeratedly gay banter was mercilessly replaced by the strains of a Perry Como record. Mary began to sing along with it while she bustled through the house, raising her voice as she went into the kitchen. She took the breakfast dishes from the table, shaking her head when she saw how much the kids had left on their plates. It hardly seemed worth giving them anything. Such a waste, with food as expensive as it was! She shook her head as she shovelled it into the pedal bin with a fork. Perry Como meandered on and Mary joined in mightily when he got to the chorus, her voice rising above the chink of plates as she washed them. When she'd finished that particular task she cleared the table, tripping over one of Jack's slippers as she did so. She glared down at the offending article for a second, making a mental note to tell him about it when he got back home that evening. No wonder the kids are untidy when their father sets them this sort of example, she thought to herself. She and Jack had been married for twenty-four -years and, not a day had gone past during that time when she hadn't had to tell him about his untidiness. He said she should stop nagging but Mary was proud of her house and how neat and tidy it was and she aimed to keep it that way. Whether the rest of the family liked it or not.

Sundays were the worst. She was always up at eight and, dead on nine, the hoover went on. The rest of the family always complained but Mary was oblivious to their protestations as she happily whizzed through the rooms with the cleaner, singing along with the radio like some demented char-lady.

Perry Como finished singing and the DJ told her it was nine o'clock. Mary dried her hands and, with the plates left on the draining rack, she scuttled upstairs to fetch the hoover.

It was the same routine every day, it never varied. Seven a.m. get up. Quarter past, get Jack and the kids up. Breakfast, get Jack off to work, make sure the kids were ready for school then, from eight fifty onwards, the house was hers. Washing up, hoovering, dusting and Mary loved every minute of it. She usually finished her housework around eleven and then she either took a trip into town (less than five minutes on the bus from the new estate) or she had coffee with one of her many friends. If there was one thing Mary enjoyed more than housework, it was a good natter.

'Did you hear about her at number 36?'

'I see so-and-so is ill.'

'Someone told me that whatsisname is having an affair with that woman, you know the one.'

But the thing which pleased her most of all was how much cleaner and tidier her house was compared to those of her friends and she felt a particular swell of pride when *they* told *her* how nice her place looked. Mary would just smile and tell them it was hard work with a family like hers but it was worth it.

Now she roared from room to room with the hoover, still singing loudly to herself despite the fact that the radio was drowned out by the din of the cleaner. She pushed it rapidly before her like some kind of jet propelled mine detector. The dusting was completed at a similarly dizzy pace and, at precisely ten fifty-three, Mary tucked her duster away neatly into a drawer and wiped her hands on her apron. However, with it being Friday, there was one more thing which she had to do. Retrieving a tin of polish from the cupboard, Mary armed herself with a fresh duster and headed out to the front doorstep.

As she opened the door, Mrs Banks from next door passed by and the two women exchanged brief pleasantries before Mary knelt to begin her last job.

It was as she took the lid off the polish that she noticed the first of the slime trails.

Mary looked at it, watching as it glinted in the sunlight. Then she saw another, and another. The whole step was criss-crossed with silver threads, some hardened the others still fresh and sticky. Mary followed the course of one fresh trail, noting that it ran across the step and up the inside of the concrete porch. On either side of the porch she had baskets of flowers and, as she stood up she saw a lump of what looked like phlegm hanging from the first of the suspended baskets. She leaned closer, peering inquisitively at the almost transparent lump but, as she looked closer she could see that the stuff was like frog-spawn only instead of being round, these things were cylindrical. With a dark centre they hung in clusters of about twenty or thirty. Mary noticed that there were five or six of these clusters on each of the hanging baskets and she felt an almost unnatural disgust as she looked at them. She told herself she must show Jack when he got home, then, careful not to touch the jellied lumps, she took her duster and knocked each one from the hanging pots.

She returned to the slime trails on the doorstep and set about removing them, polishing away feverishly until all traces of them were gone, then she closed the door. But, as she put the lid back on the polish, she wondered once more what those mucoid clusters on the flower baskets had been.

Brady brought the Vauxhall to a halt and switched off the engine. He hurriedly got out of the car, anxious to be free of its stifling confines, impatient to breathe the sweet summer air once more. He locked the door behind him and strode across the deserted street to the first of the houses he was to inspect. Elm Drive was the last street on the new estate to be filled, with families due to move in at the beginning of the following week. The council had asked him to give the houses a quick look over before the new tenants took up residence, just to make sure everything was all right. But Brady's mind was not really on his present job as he walked up the short front path to the first house. Burned deep into his mind was the image of Ron Bell's mutilated body. The police had arrived within five minutes of Archie Reece's call, the ambulance another five after that. The body had been removed by two young ambulancemen, one of whom had vomited at the scene of carnage in the old house. The local police inspector had been unable to offer much in the way of explanation, insisting that they would have to wait for the results of the autopsy before pursuing any investigation. Brady had mentioned the incident only briefly to Kim, telling her that Bell had been dead when they found him, but dispensing with the worst details of the ghoulish find.

Now he stood before the front door of number one Elm Drive, fumbling in his trouser pocket for the set of pass keys which he'd been given. His jacket was draped over his shoulder and Brady could feel the perspiration sticking to his back. The concrete of the path felt hot beneath him and he could feel its searing warmth even through the soles of his shoes. The sky was cloudless, the sun hanging there defiantly. The whole town was enveloped in a blanket of blistering heat. It was like walking about inside a huge oven.

Brady found the key ring and tried one of the keys, muttering to himself when it didn't fit the lock. He tried again.

Another failure.

He sucked in an impatient breath and pushed the third key in. This time it turned and the front door swung open. He stepped into the cloying humidity which was the hall way. The place smelt of fresh wood and his shoes beat out a tattoo on the concrete floor as he walked from room to room. He finished downstairs, did a quick tour of the upper floor and then, satisfied, moved to the next house.

He repeated the procedure in the remaining nine buildings on that side of the road, then crossed and continued his inspection of the buildings opposite.

As he entered the penultimate house, he looked up to see a couple of kids cycling past on their way to school and the Health Inspector glanced at his watch. It was almost one fifteen. After he'd finished checking these last two houses, he told himself, he'd go and get some lunch.

It was as he closed the door behind him that he saw something glinting in the rays of sunlight which fell into the hall.

Brady paused, letting go of the front door, his attention riveted to the glistening thing before him. He stepped closer, crouching slightly to get a better look.

It was a slime trail.

The front door swung back on its hinges and slammed with an almighty crash which made the Health Inspector jump. He leapt to his feet, his heart pounding.

'Shit,' he muttered, angry with himself for being so jumpy. Then he turned his attention back to the slime trail. It was dry, crumbling away when he rubbed the toe of his shoe in it. Brady followed its shiny course into the living room (or at least what would be the living room eventually), noting that there were more of the trails in the other room, one or two of them actually stretching a couple of feet up the wall. He scanned the remainder of the room then passed into the kitchen.

There were more of the trails in there.

Brady hurried out and into the last house, twisting the key almost frenziedly, pushing his way into the hall.

The slime trails were more numerous in the last house. He counted a dozen at least. For long seconds, the Health Inspector stood in the doorway, his eyes darting furtively around the humid room then he crossed to one of the trails and peered closely at it. Like the one in the house before, it was dry. Several hours, or, for all he knew, days old. All the trails were dry but Brady suddenly remembered Ron Bell and the silvery fluid which had covered his remains and he felt uneasy, suddenly anxious to be out of the house. Not really knowing why. The air seemed to be unexpectedly fetid and he hurried out into the oppressive heat once more, locking the door behind him. He crossed to his car and sat for long moments behind the wheel before leaning forward and starting the engine. He let it idle for a moment, looking at the house which he'd just left, then, with a sigh, he stuck it into first and pulled off.

Six

Bert Crossley, finished his second pint of Guinness and pushed the empty pint pot back across the bar.

'Fill that up again, Tom,' he said to the barman, fumbling in his pockets for some money. 'And whatever these two silly bastards want.' He indicated the men with him both of whom shook their heads, the first of them checking his watch.

'No thanks,' Danny said. 'I'd better be getting home, the wife will wonder where I am.' He picked up a couple of full shopping bags and left to a chorus of cheers and whistles from the few remaining occupants of the public bar. As he reached the door someone shouted, 'A woman's work is never done,' and the other men laughed loudly.

'You in a hurry too, Tony?' asked Bert Crossley, watching as the second man downed what was left in his glass.

The man nodded. 'Yeah, I'd better get back to the site. I'll see you tonight though,' he assured Bert as he left.

The big man picked up his pint and swallowed two or three enormous mouthfuls, patting his swaying belly appreciatively. He belched loudly and excused himself. Bert Crossley tipped the scales at somewhere around eighteen stone and that, combined with his height, made him a formidable sight to be propping up the bar of The Swan. Bert ran a small butcher's shop in the tiny precinct of shops situated on the new estate. The precinct also comprised a newsagent's, a small supermarket and a fish and chip shop. Bert prided himself on being the only one of the shop keepers who actually owned his own business. He stood at the bar every lunchtime between one and two p.m. nattering away about football, politics and anything else anyone would care to talk about. Putting people off their ploughman's lunches by his insistence on wearing his working apron which was perpetually stained with the rusty marks of dried blood. Considering he'd been a butcher for forty-two years, Bert still didn't seem to have mastered the use of his knives and his fingers were usually swathed in blood soaked bandages, or plasters which refused to stay on and fell off to expose a jagged gash just as someone in the bar was about to tuck into their lunch. About six years back, he'd sliced off the top of his thumb while carving up a bullock carcass but, instead of calling the ambulance, Bert had calmly closed the shop and, carrying the severed end of the digit, strolled down to the doctor's surgery. That had been when he had a shop in the town centre. He'd moved into the new premises on the estate about ten months ago and had built up a good name amongst the residents. His father had always told him that there was no substitute for the family butcher's shop and Bert had been happy to find that his old man had been right. Bert had learned all he knew about the trade from his father who used to run his own shop in the days when butchers still did their own slaughtering too. Bert remembered the first time, as a child of ten, he saw his father kill a bullock. The memory was as vivid all these years later as it was at the time. In his mind's eye he could still see his father leading the animal to the centre of the yard, tethering it to an iron post there. He remembered that the animal was drooling, saliva hanging in long white streamers from its mouth. It had stood perfectly still, almost as if it realized that there was no point in running, as Bert's father had approached it with the sledgehammer. He had steadied himself, raising the heavy hammer above his head. Then, with a blow combining demonic force and years of practice, he'd brought the sledge down on the bullock's head. There was a strident snapping of bone as the skull was shattered, the beast pitching forward as its front legs buckled. It had been dead before it hit the floor. Bert had then watched as his father had hung it up, sliced open the throat to drain it and then set about cutting the animal up. He had watched it all in fascination, remembering the smells too. The overpowering smell of the blood and the pungent odour of excrement which flowed out in a trail behind the twitching beast as his father had dragged it away with a meat hook.

Bert downed the rest of his pint and sighed wistfully. There'd been an art to butchering in those days. It still needed a lot of skill, granted, but the art was gone. Now the livestock were slaughtered hundreds in a day by the pneumatic gun which shot a retractable bolt into their heads. The carcasses arrived at the butcher's in storage lorries, already prepared. The only skill that remained was in cutting the damn things up.

'Another one, Bert?' asked the barman, reaching for the empty pint pot.

The butcher shook his head. 'No thanks, Tom, I'd better get back and open up.' He glanced at the clock above the bar. It was almost two o'clock. He got to his feet and lumbered out into the sunshine, wiping his face with the back of his hand. Bert perspired a lot, even in relatively cool weather, but today he thought he must have lost a couple of pounds already. He glanced up at the blazing sun and began the short walk from the pub to the shop. It took him past some old people's flats and one or two of the old dears waved gaily to Bert as he passed. He was a popular man with all the residents and many found it a surprise that he had never married but, throughout his life, Bert had always found that his business was more important than the ties of a home life. After his father died, he'd looked after his mother, nursing her through her last few painful years until she had a stroke which proved to be fatal. By that time Bert was forty-one. He had his business and, what was more, he just thought he was too old to start chasing women around.

A fly buzzed past him, attracted by the dried blood on his apron but Bert shooed it away. He reached the back door of the shop and let himself in. It was much cooler in there and he stood beneath one of the powerful fans for a moment before walking through into the shop itself. The blinds were down so the shop was in a kind of semi-darkness. Bert was about to pull them up when something made him turn to face the display cabinets.

His mouth dropped open and, for once, he was speechless.

When he had left the shop at one o'clock, less than an hour ago, the cabinets had been full. Their trays heaped with fine cuts of beef, pork, lamb, kidneys, liver. Everything. Now, Bert ran disbelieving eyes over the remnants of his stock. The meat and offal had been devoured, only tiny scraps of it remained in the stainless steel trays. Even the blood which had run from the meat was gone, every last drop removed as if by some invisible hand. There were pieces of meat on the floor too, here and there were some dark patches of blood.

Bert put a hand to his forehead, drawing in a long, slow breath.

'My God,' he murmured softly. Then, immediately, his bewilderment turned to anger. Who the hell would do such a thing? He quickly inspected the locks on the doors and windows. If some bastard had broken in Bert promised himself he'd gut the sod personally. But a swift inspection told him that the doors and windows were still secure.

He stood silently, gazing at the empty trays before him, wondering if maybe he'd had too much to drink that lunch time and he was really imagining this.

'My God,' he muttered once more.

The shop was silent but for the bluebottle which buzzed indolently around him. Bert decided to check the back door and windows and he hurried through to the rear of the building.

In his haste he failed to notice the slime trails which led from the display cabinets to the ventilator grille on the wall. Still fresh, they glittered with a vile sparkle of their own.

Seven

Brady wiped his face with a handkerchief as he walked across the car park towards the council offices. The café where he usually had his lunch was only 200 yards from the large building and could be seen from his own office window. He looked in that direction as he crossed the car park. Christ, it was hot. The tarmac beneath his feet looked as though it was on the verge of bubbling. Brady hadn't eaten much, the experience in the two new houses had quelled his appetite but he pushed the incident to the back of his mind. The Health Inspector loosened his tie as he wearily climbed the flight of stone steps to the main doors, the sun burning fiercely on his back as he turned to enter the building.

It was cool in there and he managed to ignore the frightful rattle emitted by one defective fan. The sound reminded him of a football rattle. As he crossed reception on the way to the staircase, Julie Jenkins called him across to the desk. Brady turned, running an appraising eye over the youngest staff member in the building. She was in her early twenties and had only been working there for three months but, already, most people seemed to have taken to her. The male members of the work-force in particular. She smiled sweetly at Brady who returned the gesture, managing a quick glance at her shapely figure as he did so. Because of the hot weather she wore only a light, cheese-cloth top through which he glimpsed the dark outline of her nipples straining against the flimsy material. The blouse was undone to the third button to reveal a tiny silver crucifix hanging between her ample breasts. Brady smiled to himself, administering a swift mental rebuke for taking so much interest in a girl young enough to be his daughter. Anyway, he told himself, you're a married man. Nevertheless, just because you've bought the goods doesn't stop you window shopping, he mused.

Julie held up a piece of paper, smiling as Brady leant on the reception desk.

'A message for you·, Mr Brady,' she told him. 'A lady rang up to complain about her drains and toilet.'

'Blockage?' asked the Health Inspector.

Julie nodded.

'Then it's a job for the sewage department, not me.'

'She says that there's a terrible smell coming from the drains. She wants it checked.' Julie looked at him, the deep blue of her eyes reminding Brady of the sky outside.

He sighed. 'OK. What's the name and address?'

She handed him the piece of paper and the Health Inspector pushed it into his pocket.

'It's on the new estate,' said Julie, as if she was telling him something he didn't know.

Brady exhaled deeply. 'Well, I can think of better ways of spending an afternoon than bending over drains and toilets, especially in this sort of weather.' He smiled. 'Give the sewage people a buzz anyway. I might need one of their blokes along, just in case it's anything below the surface.' He turned and headed towards the staircase.

Julie flicked a switch on the console before her, picking up the phone when a green light flickered on.

Brady reached his office and walked in to find the heat almost unbearable. He crossed to the window and heaved it up, allowing a blast of cool air to blow in. The perspiration beneath his arms and on his back suddenly felt very cold but he remained at the window, looking down on the people in the car park, as they scuttled around in the heat with their bags of shopping. All of them were probably complaining about the heat. Brady smiled to himself. When it was the depth of winter everyone longed for the summer but when *that* finally arrived they spent their time cursing the heat. He was the same. A knock on the office door broke his chain of thought.

50

'Come in,' he called, turning to face his visitor.

The door opened and a short stocky man in white overalls walked in. He smiled at Brady and introduced himself as Don Palmer. The Health Inspector caught the slightest hint of a cockney accent in the man's voice.

'You're from the sewage department?' he asked, although it came out more as a statement than a question.

Palmer nodded. 'That's right, guv. They call us "Effluent Operatives".' He smiled, broadly. A warm, infectious grin which caused Brady to smile too. 'Well,' he said, holding up a bag of tools. 'I've got my plunger. Shall we go?'

Brady followed the little man down to the car park where a white van with MERTON URBAN DISTRICT COUNCIL emblazoned on the sides was parked. Palmer hopped behind the steering wheel, Brady told him where to go and they set off.

Brady wound down the window of the van and allowed some cool air to blow in, and also to drive away the smoke from Palmer's cigarette which filled the van. The little man retrieved a packet of Marlboro from the parcel shelf and pointed it in the Health Inspector's direction.

'I don't smoke,' said Brady. 'Thanks all the same.'

'Wish *I* could give up,' said Palmer. 'It costs me about ten quid a week for fags.' He took a last drag and tossed the butt out of the open window. 'I've been smoking ever since I was eleven, doubt if I'll ever manage to kick it now. My old lady keeps on at me to stop but, well, you know how it is.'

'Which part of London are you from?' Brady asked, studying his companion's profile.

The little man laughed. 'Christ, is my accent *that* strong?'

The Health Inspector smiled. 'Well, let's say it's noticeable.'

'Islington,' Palmer told him.

'What did you do there?'

'Same as I do here. Effluent operative.' He laughed once more. 'Bloody stupid name isn't it? I don't know why they can't just call us shit-shovellers. They called us flushers when I worked in the London sewers.' A wistful grin passed across his face. 'I used to do a bit of boxing before that, only amateur like. When I was a kid.'

'Why did you give up?' Brady wanted to know.

'The old lady again. She was scared I might get brain damage or something,' Palmer explained.

'Did you get very far?' the Health Inspector asked, his interest genuinely aroused by this personable little man in the white overalls.

Palmer shrugged. 'I got to the final of the ABA light weight competition one year. Albert Hall. Thousands of people there, millions watching on TV.'

'How did you get on?' Brady wanted to know.

'Well, I had the geezer worried in the third round.'

Brady was impressed. 'Yeah?'

Palmer nodded. 'Yeah.' He paused. 'He thought he'd killed me.' The little man cracked out laughing, the raucous sound filling the van and Brady chuckled too.

'What made you move to Merton?' the Health Inspector wanted to know.

'London's all right for grown-ups but I didn't want my kids living in all that smog,' Palmer explained. 'I wanted them to get up every morning and breathe fresh air instead of bloody diesel fumes.' He glanced at Brady. 'You got any kids?'

'No,' said the Health Inspector, just a little too sharply.

Palmer looked at him for a second then turned his attention back to the road ahead.

Brady changed the subject quickly. 'I used to work in London too.'

Palmer smiled. 'Yeah? Same job?'

Brady nodded.

'Why did *you* move?'

'That's something even I've never been able to work out,' he confessed. 'I think things just got on top of me. Besides, I was doing all the work in the department. I thought that if I left the other lazy bastards would have to start pulling their weight.'

The sewage man nodded.

'What the hell makes a bloke start in a business like yours?' Brady asked. 'I mean, crawling about in...' He hesitated.

'Crawling about in other people's shit. Was that what you were going to say?' asked Palmer.

Brady laughed, nodding.

Palmer shrugged. 'Well, look at it this way. It's a secure job. I mean, unless there's a mass outbreak of constipation, I've always got plenty to do.' He laughed his cackling laugh once more. 'There's a lot of difference between working these shite-pipes and working the ones in London,' he explained. 'I mean, the ones here are small, you have to crawl along the bloody things on all fours. At least in London you could walk through them.'

Brady frowned at the prospect.

Palmer suddenly slowed up. 'What was that address again?'

The Health Inspector found the piece of paper and scanned it.

'Twenty-two Acacia Avenue,' he said, looking out of the window to see that they had, in fact, arrived. Both men got out of the van, Brady leading the way to the front door. He saw one of the curtains parted slightly, a face peering out inquisitively from behind dirty net. He rang the doorbell and a two-tone Woolworth's chime tinkled. The two men waited, listening as several bolts were drawn back and Palmer suppressed a smile. The door opened a fraction and a woman squinted out at them, staying in the shadows, almost as if she were reluctant to feel the sun on her face.

'Mrs Fortune?' asked Brady, smiling.

The woman, who he guessed was well into her seventies, ran an appraising eye over the two newcomers.

'We're from the council. You rang about your drains,' the Health Inspector continued, still smiling. When he got no answer, he began to wonder if the woman was deaf so he raised his voice and repeated himself.

'All right,' she squawked. 'There's no need to shout. They're round the back.'

Brady nodded and was about to say something else when the front door was slammed in his face. He looked at Palmer who was laughing quietly. The two men made their way around to the rear of the house where Mrs Fortune appeared at the back door, this time emerging into the yard itself. She was a short, tubby woman, her hair done up in a bun, with horn-rimmed glasses perched precariously on the end of her nose. But the most striking thing about her was her clothes. She was wearing a huge knitted cardigan which came to well below her knees and looked as if it could have doubled as a bedspread and Brady could just detect the faint smell of mothballs.

'It's the drains,' she said, crisply.

Brady followed her pointing finger to the drain just below her kitchen window. As he stepped past her, a stench so fetid as to be obscene hit him and he recoiled. It reminded him of something between rotten vegetables and dead fish.

'Jesus Christ,' he groaned, watching as Palmer knelt beside the foul smelling drain. The sewage man pulled a pair of thick gloves from his overall pocket and slipped them on. He seemed impervious to the nauseating stench and beckoned Brady forward. The Health Inspector put a handkerchief over his nose to keep out the worst of the odour but it was so rank that it seemed to penetrate the very material itself. As he watched, Palmer took a long, hook-like implement from his canvas bag and poked it through the holes in the grate. He stirred it about, finally lifting the grille, uncovering the drain opening. There were pieces of rotten cabbage and what looked like congealed grease around the opening and Palmer scooped them away with one hand, peering closer.

'I think it's disgusting,' said Mrs Fortune, indignantly. 'Fancy letting the drains get in such a state. Why haven't the council done anything before?'

'This is the first complaint we've had from anyone on the new estate,' Brady told her, stepping back from the foul smelling opening.

She grunted indignantly.

'You say that your toilet is blocked too?' he asked her.

'Yes,' she snapped. 'It has been for more than a day now.'

'But how do…'

'It's only the outside one,' she snapped. 'The one upstairs is all right.' She pointed to a green door away to the right and Brady crossed to it, peering inside. The outside toilet was almost on the point of overflowing, the water already up to just below the seat. Brady closed the door and walked back into the yard.

Palmer had a torch out now and was shining it down the open drain. He finally switched it off and stood up.

'Well, I can't see anything,' he said. 'There's no external reason for the blockage or the smell.' He fumbled in his bag once more, closely watched by Brady and Mrs Fortune. The sewage man finally produced several lengths of steel tubing to which he attached what looked like a small grappling hook. Carefully, he pushed the long probe down into the drain, hearing it clanking against the metal of the pipe as he pushed further.

'I think it's disgusting,' Mrs Fortune said once more and, with a disdainful shrug of her shoulders, she disappeared back into the house, slamming the door behind her.

'I bet she doesn't offer us a cup of tea,' said Palmer, still threading the metal probe into the drainpipe. He looked across at Brady and winked.

'How the hell can you stand that stink?' asked the Health Inspector.

'I must admit,' said Palmer, 'this one is a bit worse than usual but I'll be buggered if I can think what's causing it. It must be pretty deep down whatever it is.' He suddenly stiffened and the metal rod seemed to quiver in his hand. The little man gripped the rod tight, pressing one foot against the drain surround to steady himself. The tugging continued.

'What the fuck...' the sentence trailed off.

'What's wrong?' asked Brady, suddenly alarmed by the expression on Palmer's face.

The little man was straining to tug the rod free, using every ounce of his strength to pull it from the drain.

Brady crossed to help him, fixing both hands around the probe. He felt a similar pressure being exerted from the other end.

It felt as if someone was trying to pull the rod from their hands.

'Can you feel that?' asked Palmer.

Brady nodded, anxiously. Then, finally, with a concerted burst of strength, the two men managed to heave the rod free. It came up, bringing with it a lump of brown matter. Brady looked at the lump which appeared to be a very old apple.

'Could that have been causing the blockage?' he asked.

Palmer shook his head, studying the probe closely. He sighed thoughtfully then had a quick look in the outside toilet. That done, he crossed to an iron flap which lay about ten yards down the garden. There was a disgusting smell emanating from there too. He stood on the sewer cover as if seeking inspiration.

'Whatever's causing the block is very deep,' he said. 'I can't clear it from this end".'

Brady looked apprehensive. 'Meaning?'

'Meaning, we'll have to go down.' He pointed at the rusty cover which led down into the sewer itself. 'You wait here,' he told the Health Inspector. 'I'll go and get the stuff from the van.'

Brady stood beside the flap, waving a hand before him in an effort to keep the rancid stench at bay. He heard Palmer's footsteps receding as he disappeared around the side of the house to fetch 'the stuff - whatever the hell that might be.

He didn't have to wait long for an answer. A moment later, the little man re-appeared carrying two thick bundles of clothing and another canvas bag which he deposited on the ground.

'Put that on,' he said to Brady, pushing one of the bundles towards him. The Health Inspector picked up the bundle and opened it out, realizing that it was an overall of some kind. Made of oilskin, it looked like a shiny white boiler suit. It fastened up the front by a zip which, in turn, was covered with a flap which both men clipped together using the large press-studs along its length. At the back, Brady found that the folds of the material could be pulled up to form a hood which was, in turn, tied at the chin with a piece of cord. As he pulled the hood up, all the sounds around him became muffled and he looked up to see a bird sitting on a nearby tree apparently whistling noiselessly. Its song could not be heard through the thick protective headgear. He pulled on the heavy gloves which Palmer handed him, watching as the little man knelt beside the other canvas bag. He finally produced a pair of large boots which Brady found he could slip over his shoes quite easily. The soles were metal and, for a moment, he found himself rooted to the spot by the weight.

The last things which Palmer took from his bag of tricks were a couple of face masks, rather like those worn by scuba divers, only curved and covering the whole of the face. Brady put his on, his breath coming in short gasps, the smell of plastic making him feel dizzy. The heat was almost unbearable. There was a small, circular, hole at the base of the mask which, Palmer informed him, was an air filter. The little man had to raise his voice to make Brady hear. The Health Inspector's breathing had slowed now, rasping loudly in the mask as he stood watching the other man.

'We've got to get this off,' shouted Palmer, his voice still sounding slightly muffled. It was as if he were talking through cotton wool. He pointed to the metal flap which covered the sewer opening and Brady looked down at the knobbed metal. Rusted with the ravages of the weather, it had two depressions in it. One at either end, both of which had a bar across them. At a signal from Palmer, both men bent, hooked their fingers under the bars and lifted.

The lid to the sewer opening came free and they deposited it on the grass nearby.

Palmer handed a torch to the Health Inspector who peered down into the darkness. It seemed to be bottomless, the iron ladder which ran down the side of the shaft disappearing into gloom so total that even the torch beams could not penetrate it for more than a couple of feet.

The sewage man looked at Brady, who was still gazing down into the darkness, and then stooped to pick up his bag of tools which he clipped to his belt.

'Last one in's a rotten egg,' he said, raising his voice once more to make himself heard. He smiled, then, watched by the Health Inspector, he clambered onto the ladder and began to make his way down into the darkness, visible, finally, only by his swaying torch beam.

Brady flicked on his own torch, took one last look around at the brightness of the day and then lowered himself onto the first rung of the ladder, his metal soled boots clanking noisily as he did so.

He steadied himself for a second, then began to descend.

Eight

Brady hadn't realized quite how narrow the shaft was until he began to climb down the ladder. Now he found that he was forced to cling tightly to the metal rungs in order to prevent his back rubbing against the other side of the tunnel. The torch wavered unsteadily in his hand and his mask had begun to cloud over, making it difficult to see. He measured his steps cautiously, careful not to miss a rung and fall. However, despite his tentative tread, he felt his left foot slide from the rung beneath him and, for a moment, his heart leapt. But he gripped the ladder tighter and continued his descent.

He heard a dull splash, signalling to him that Palmer had reached the bottom of the shaft and, a moment later, Brady himself felt his heavy boot touching something solid which he knew to be the floor of the pipe. Panting, he stood still for a moment until he felt hands tugging at his arm.

'Mind your head,' Palmer told him, shining the torch around to show him the narrowness of the pipe.

Brady guessed that it could be no more than three and a half feet from the top to bottom and both men had to get on all fours to give themselves the room to move about in it. Brady sank reluctantly to his knees, looking down to see that the trickling effluent which ran through the pipe came up as far as his forearms. He felt sick and was thankful that he had the mask on. The walls of the pipe seemed to crush in on him and the Health Inspector imagined that this was what it was like to be buried alive. Together, he and Palmer crawled through what seemed like an endless cylindrical coffin, thick with human waste and twelve instead of six feet below ground. The heat inside the suit seemed to intensify and Brady found that he was gasping for air even though the mask was filtering it quite adequately.

'You all right?' Palmer asked him, hearing the Health Inspector's laboured, accelerated breathing. He peered over his shoulder at his companion, shining the torch at him.

Brady nodded, his breathing becoming less harsh. The perspiration was running off him and he almost slipped twice, the thought of ending up face first in a river of human excreta making him more careful.

In the darkness, neither of the men saw three or four of the slugs glide past them, carried along by the flow.

Palmer held up a hand for Brady to halt. The little man managed to scramble up onto his knees in front of a grille which was set into the tunnel roof.

'What's that?' asked Brady.

'It's the outlet from the toilet,' Palmer told him, fumbling in his bag for a screwdriver. He set to work, removing the four rusty screws which held the grille in position. As he took each one out, he handed it to Brady to hold, then, when the last one was out, he stuck the end of the screwdriver between two bars of the grille and prised it free. By torchlight he scrutinised it.

'No blockage there,' he said, puzzled.

'What now?' Brady asked, peering up the outlet.

Palmer grinned. 'We hope the old girl doesn't get taken short.'

The Health Inspector quickly withdrew his head, handing the screws, one at a time, to the sewage man who refixed the grille.

'Let's have a look at the drain outlet,' said Palmer and, pointing his torch ahead of him, crawled on. Brady followed.

'Are all the tunnels as narrow as this?' he asked.

'Most of them,' Palmer told him. 'They all work like wheels though. The pipes themselves converge in one central chamber, which is like the hub of the wheel. The tunnels are like the spokes.' He paused for a moment, steadying himself as he put his hand on something thick and soft. He grunted distastefully. He crawled on.

The large slug which Palmer had accidentally put his hand on slithered along the floor of the pipe, the stream of effluent and the impenetrable darkness hiding it.

'The manhole covers that you see in the road,' the sewage man continued. 'Each one of those goes down to one of the central chambers. They're dotted all over town. The chambers are pretty big.' The little man stopped once more, this time at a much smaller outlet which Brady realized must be the one from the drain. The same procedure was repeated, the grille removed. This time a lump of rotten potato fell out into Palmer's gloved hand. He shook his head and dropped it into the stream of effluent.

'I don't get it,' he said. 'Even down here there's nothing to show why the bloody pipes are blocked. 'He pulled a curved implement from his bag and began scraping around in the drain outlet. Brady meanwhile shone his torch around the walls of the pipe. About half-way up the sides there was a scum mark of green mould which, in places, had extended to the roof of the pipe too. The concrete itself seemed to be cracked and the mould had crept into the rent like bacteria into a cut, turning it gangrenous. He remembered when he had found an old man living alone who had been infected with gangrene. Unable to move after falling and cutting his leg, Brady had found him after a next door neighbour complained about the smell coming from the man's house. He'd finally got in to discover that the old boy's leg was green and mottled with infection, black in places it was so bad. That image suddenly came to his mind as he ran the torch up the tunnel wall, following the course of the rent until it reached the roof of the tunnel. The torch beam shone on something silvery.

Brady felt the breath catch in his throat as he looked more closely. The marks were unmistakable.

The roof of the pipe was criss-crossed by dozens of slime trails.

Ron Bell's house. The two houses in Elm Drive and now here. With shaking hand he reached up and touched one of the trails with the index finger of his glove. The mucoid fluid stuck to the material, dropping away in thick globules when Brady removed his hand. Suddenly anxious, he shone the torch down the length of the tunnel but the beam faded into darkness less than three feet from him. Something bumped against his arm and he almost shouted aloud. Looking down he saw that it was a small piece of wood. His breathing once again became rapid but he tried to control it, clenching his teeth until his jaws ached. Get a bloody grip on yourself, he screamed inside his head. Come on. He clenched his fists, his eyes tightly closed for long seconds, then he felt Palmer touch him on the shoulder.

'Well,' said the sewage man. 'I can't find anything. We might as well go back up.'

The words were the most welcome Brady had heard in a long time. He crawled backwards (it was impossible to turn round in the narrow pipe) until his torch glinted on the bottom rung of the ladder. High above, he could see the blue of the sky and, with almost unnatural haste, he began to clamber up towards the surface.

Palmer waited at the bottom of the ladder, watching as Brady climbed up. When the Health Inspector was half way up, the little man followed him.

He didn't even see the large slug which had crawled onto his boot.

As he climbed, the slug crept higher, sensing the warmth beneath the overalls. It slithered onto his calf and prepared to sink its long central tooth into the material, eager to get at the warm flesh beneath. But, just then, Palmer brought his foot down particularly hard on the ladder, the slug lost its hold and fell back into the stream of waste below.

The sewage man heard the splash and thought he'd dropped something from his bag. He shone his torch down but could see nothing. Satisfied that he still had all his tools, he continued his ascent.

The slug had disappeared.

Nine

The heat hung heavily over Merton, like some oppressive cloud. As the afternoon wore on and the sun reached its zenith, the little town was bathed in a cloying, sticky heat which seemed to make the air itself hot, almost unbreathable.

Carol Wilton stood naked before the full length mirror studying the reflection which gazed back at her. Her eyelids felt heavy and she was tired, the heat seeming to sap her strength. Beads of perspiration had formed on her top lip and she licked them away, the salty taste remaining on her tongue momentarily. Another bead of clear liquid quivered at the hollow of her throat for a second before trickling slowly down her chest, between her taut breasts and across her flat stomach. She traced its path with the index finger of her right hand, allowing the digit to probe deeper, brushing through the soft curls of her pubic hair. She shuddered as the finger brushed against her clitoris and she felt a tingle run through her. She sighed, her nipples rising to erection at the same time. Carol moved her finger gently between her legs, feeling the first traces of moisture from her warm cleft. All the time she kept her eyes firmly on the mirror, watching the reflection before her. She parted her lips slightly and spoke one word.

'Tony.'

She stopped moving her finger, her expression changing from one of pleasure to one of anger.

'You bastard,' she said softly, withdrawing her finger.

Couldn't she forget him after four years? She shook herself out of her dream world and crossed to the bed, reaching for a pair of faded jeans which she pulled on, the tight material clinging to her slim hips and thighs. She slid further into the denims, allowing the seam to cut into her damp cleft, then she fastened the button and picked up the white t-shirt which also lay on the bed. She let it hang outside her jeans, noting how the thin material made her hardened nipples even more prominent. She slipped on a pair of backless high heels and inspected the reflection once more. You should see me now, you bastard, she thought. The image of Tony flashed into her mind once more. No, she couldn't forget him. He'd left her a permanent reminder just to make sure. She crossed to the bedroom window and looked out.

Paul was playing on the lawn, sitting contentedly beside the rabbit's pen, watching as the small white creature hopped about, stopping every now and then to munch on the pieces of lettuce which Carol had dropped in half an hour ago. Paul was four now and he'd never even seen his father. Carol watched him and felt the anger rising once more inside her. Fate had dealt her a truly cruel blow. Not only had she been left to bring up a child on her own, the child had been born slightly retarded. She bit her bottom lip, angrily. It was almost as if she blamed Tony for her son's mental deficiency. But the real anger she felt was with herself. God, she'd been a fool in those days. A sixteen-year-old girl trying to act like a woman. Tony had been twenty-four. She'd built her world around him, ignoring the warnings from her parents and friends. What did they know? He loved her and she used to show them the gifts he bought her to prove it. He loved her and she loved him. He took her virginity but she didn't care, she had given it up willingly. She had talked about getting married, though he never seemed to take much interest when it got around to that subject but then, she had told herself, not many men do talk about marriage. They made love often and he guided her, taught her things she had never even known about, introduced her to all manner of physical pleasure. And she had accepted it all. She loved him and that was all that mattered to her.

But then she became pregnant and Tony changed. They rowed constantly and, finally, he had given her his ultimatum. Get an abortion or the relationship was over. He even offered to pay for it himself.

She refused. He left her.

'Bastard,' she muttered to herself, the memory still hurting even four years later.

Of course her parents had gone through the customary procedure of disowning her. Being Catholics in a religious area didn't help matters, she supposed. Whatever would the neighbours say? How could you do such a thing, Carol? The recriminations had flown back and forth and she'd moved out. First to a flat and finally to this house she had now, on the new estate. She'd left school at sixteen with no qualifications but she'd managed to get a cleaning job at the local hospital. The meagre wages from that, together with her supplementary benefit and child allowance just about paid the rent and kept her and the child in food and clothes. With Paul being handicapped, the Government, in its infinite wisdom, saw fit to give her an extra couple of quid on top of the usual rate. And so she managed. At times she wondered how but things never got too desperate. She'd made lots of new friends on the estate, one of whom looked after Paul while Carol went out to work at nights. Back to her old job at the hospital. She sometimes wondered what it would have been like if Tony had stayed with her. Would she have been a wife by now instead of an unmarried mother, disowned by her own family? Many a night she lay awake wanting him with her. But recently, she wouldn't have cared *who* it was who shared her bed.

She pushed the thoughts to one side and made her way downstairs. Paul didn't hear her as she walked up behind him and he giggled when she tickled his ribs. He looked up at her with wide, questioning eyes for a second, almost as if he didn't recognise her. Then he gurgled something unintelligible and returned his attention to the small rabbit. Carol knelt beside him and wiped some saliva from his mouth with the tissue which she took from her jeans pocket. He didn't move, his mind still pre-occupied with the tiny white animal hopping about before him. Carol had bought it about a week ago and the man next door had helped make a pen for it. A nice bloke, Carol thought. Pity he was married. The rabbit had been an endless source of fascination for Paul and Carol could now leave him out in the garden all day, just watching the little creature.

'Paul,' she said, stroking his hair. It was blond, like her own. Soft and sleek as she touched it.

'Paul.' She gently turned his head so that he was looking at her. Once more she was faced with that vacant expression. 'Mummy's just going out for five minutes,' she told him, reaching once more for the tissue. She wiped the mucus from his nose and balled up the tissue. 'Will you be all right?'

He smiled. 'Yes,' he said, quickly. Shaking his head about. 'Yes.'

'You watch bunny, all right?' she said. 'Mummy be back in five minutes.'

'Yes,' he said again, looking back at the rabbit. He raised one chubby hand and waved in the direction of the animal. 'Bunny.'

Carol smiled. 'That's right, bunny.' She kissed him on the forehead and walked back up the garden to the house. Her purse was on the kitchen table and she opened it to reveal a pound note, some silver and an assortment of other stuff including a bus ticket, a coupon cut from a newspaper which granted her 3p off her next purchase of a certain brand of tea bag and a couple of photos. The sort taken in photo booths. The faded monochrome snaps showed her and Tony together. She snapped her purse together again and left the house. The precinct of shops was only down the road and she needed some bread and a pint of milk. Thank Christ the Giro is due in the morning, she thought.

Paul heard the clicking of his mother's heels as she walked up the path and out of the gate but he didn't turn to watch her go. He was too interested in the rabbit. He gurgled contentedly, the spittle oozing down his chin and forming a silvery pendant as it hung there.

The rabbit had stopped to eat and it crouched before him devouring the remnants of the lettuce which it had been given. But suddenly, it jumped back, licking at its paw.

Paul laughed, throatily, watching the animal. He could see something red on its fur, on the paw it was licking but he didn't know what it was. Neither did he realize what the slimy black thing was that burrowed slowly up from the place where the rabbit had been crouching.

The slug pulled itself free of the ground and slid across the ground towards the rabbit, its antennae waving about in the air, the shorter forward tentacles flicking across the ground.

The rabbit watched the slug warily for a second and was about to leap aside when it squealed in pain. It managed to drag itself a few inches and this time, Paul saw one of the monstrous black things clinging to the animal's leg. The rabbit turned and bit into the second slug but the first and larger of the creatures had reached it by now and the terrified mammal was pulled down as the slug fastened itself onto one of the rabbit's ears. Blood ran freely from the wound as the slug used its sharp row of radular teeth to shave off pieces of the animal's flesh.

Another slug, fully six inches long, broke the surface, dragging its vile form towards the stricken rabbit. It drove its sickle shaped tooth into the animal's side and the fur was suddenly stained crimson. The rabbit shook its head madly from side to side in an effort to dislodge the monstrous black thing but its efforts were useless and now half a dozen of the revolting gastropods were burrowing up from beneath it, each slithering across to join the attack. The rabbit tried to move but its tiny form was weighed down and all it could do was squeal as the slugs ate it alive.

Paul watched, mesmerised, his mouth open. Once he chuckled, not really knowing why but then he wrinkled his forehead as he saw the rabbit being reduced to a blood-spattered heap of fur. It had stopped moving and the slugs seethed over it, eager for the taste of its fresh, warm blood. One of its ears was eaten away, the other severed half way up. It hung uselessly, like a broken twig and, finally, the rabbit was pulled to the ground, its bloody fur almost invisible beneath the black mass of feeding slugs.

Paul gurgled as he watched, his head on one side.

Carol glanced down the garden as she walked round the house into the back garden. She looked down and saw Paul, still staring into the rabbit pen. Carol took her small bag of groceries into the house and put them on the kitchen table then she kicked off her shoes and padded down the garden towards her son, who, apparently hadn't heard her return.

'Paul,' she called but he didn't turn and it was then that Carol realized something was wrong.

She couldn't see the rabbit.

Hurrying down to the pen she stopped behind Paul, looking at the sight before her. The grass inside the pen was covered in blood and pieces of fur, here she noticed a lump of bone, beside it a piece of intestine. She turned away and closed her eyes, trying not to be sick. Gradually she regained control and looked more closely at the scene of carnage in the pen. The rabbit had disappeared completely.

Carol knelt beside Paul and held him tightly in her arms but he seemed unconcerned. He waved a hand towards the empty pen and shook his head.

'What happened?' she asked him, tears in her eyes. She glanced at the blood-stained grass once more and this time she caught sight of the mucoid fluid which also covered the pen. It sparkled in the sunlight, diffusing into a dozen different colours.

'Paul,' she repeated, holding him close to her.

He gurgled something and at first she thought he said 'cat', but when he spoke again she was able to make out the word.

'Black,' he said in his clumsy, clipped tones. He waved towards the pools of blood and slime.

'Black.'

Ten

The sun was bleeding to death in the evening sky, flooding the heavens with vivid patches of gold and crimson. Some of them eventually darkening into a cool purple as the evening drew in. Birds returning to their nests were black arrowheads against the red back-drop and the mottled sky was like a child's colouring book, layers of colour splashed brilliantly one on top of the other.

Harold Morris looked up from the begonia he was tending and marvelled at the multi-hued glory of the dusky heavens. there was nothing in the world he liked more than to be out in his greenhouse on an evening like this. Even beneath the canopy of glass and wood, the air had cooled to a pleasing temperature and Harold worked enthusiastically over his plants, tending them with a care which people usually reserve for small children.

He'd always been a keen gardener but since being made redundant from Merton's chemical works over a year ago he'd turned his hobby into something approaching an obsession. The greenhouse had been purchased with part of the sizeable pay-off he'd received. The remainder had gone into the house, new carpets and, for the first time during their thirty years' marriage, a colour television. Harold's wife, Jean, was totally mesmerised by the new acquisition something which Harold himself was thankful for because it kept her out of his way while he tended to his plants. The rest of his redundancy payment had gone towards purchasing two tickets for a flight to Australia.

Their only daughter had emigrated, with her husband, six years ago and now Harold and Jean were preparing themselves to fly over for the christening of their grandson in just under a month.

Harold smiled happily at the thought, dropping some Baby-Bio into a pot where he was nurturing an orchid.

As well as flowering plants he also had a sizeable choice of vegetables growing in the greenhouse and, together with those in the patch at the bottom of the garden, Jean seldom had to buy any from the shops. Apart from his cucumbers and tomatoes, Harold had also been able to grow a fair crop of aubergines. They were his particular pride and joy.

He sipped slowly from the tin of lager beside him, putting the can down beside a set of shears which lay on the work top. Then, picking up his trowel, Harold set about re-potting some geraniums.

The sun had fallen far below the horizon by now and night was seeping slowly across the sky, staining the clouds like ink on blotting paper. Harold squinted in the gloom for a few more minutes then crossed to the light switch at the end of the greenhouse and snapped it on. The bank of fluorescents flickered into life bathing the place in a cold white light. He then adjusted the thermostat control, raising the temperature just four or five degrees. He picked up the can of lager and drained the last dregs, rattling the empty receptacle in his hand before tossing it into the bin beneath the work top. He looked at his watch and decided that he had time to finish tending to the fresh crop of tomatoes before he went inside to watch the football.

It was almost ten p.m. and Harold felt like another can of lager. It was warm in the greenhouse and he had worked up a powerful thirst. He pulled off his gloves and dropped them onto the work-top, then he headed up the garden towards the house.

From beneath the bottom of the work top, the first of the three slugs slithered up, its posterior tentacles waving about. Moving slowly in their mucoid trails, the black beasts, one of them as thick as a man's index finger, crawled over the trowel leaving their mark on it. They paused at the place where Harold had left his gloves and then, after a moment's hesitation, they slithered inside. Harold found Jean dozing in her chair, the TV still on at full blast as yet another American cop series drew mercifully to a close. He stood in the doorway of the sitting room, rolling the icy can of lager across his forehead. Jean seemed to sense his presence and opened her eyes. She looked round and smiled.

'I thought you were busy with your plants,' she said, yawning.

'And I thought you were *watching* that,' he said, motioning towards the TV.

Jean reached for the remote control and turned down the sound.

'I nodded off,' she confessed. 'It must be this heat.'

'It'll be lot hotter than this in Australia,' he told her, sipping at his lager.

Jean sighed wistfully. 'You know, Harry, I still can't believe we're going to see Roger and Carol again.' She smiled. 'And the little boy too. Won't it be marvellous?'

'You'll be telling me next you were pleased I got made redundant,' he said, smiling.

She held out a hand to him and he bent and kissed her on the top of the head.

'Will you be much longer?' she asked him.

Harold shook his head. 'I'll be hurrying in to you my dear,' he said, bowing exaggeratedly.

'And the football,' she said, smiling.

He winked at her and walked out. The cool evening air seemed full of the scent of flowers and Harold inhaled deeply. In next door's garden he heard a snuffling sound and, a second later, saw a hedgehog scuttle across the lawn ahead of him, trying its best to avoid the light coming from the greenhouse.

Stars stuck to the black velvet sky like pieces of tinsel which some giant hand had hurled. Harold smiled to himself and pushed open the door to the greenhouse, the temperature immediately hitting him. He hadn't realized just how hot it was in there but, after a moment or two and a hefty pull from his lager can, he re-adjusted to the heat and looked at the waiting tomatoes.

He reached for his gloves.

Yes, the tomatoes were coming along beautifully this year, he thought, pulling on the first of his gloves. Last year's crop had...

He stopped trying to drag the second glove on, feeling something wet and slimy blocking the fingers.

'What the hell...'

He never finished the sentence. Suddenly, searing pain exploded through his hand as three sets of jaws fastened themselves on his exposed fingers. The slugs inside the glove eagerly devoured the flesh offered to them, quickly tearing it away until they were nearing the very bone itself. Harold was frantic, his bulging eyes watched the material of the glove undulating rhythmically as blood began to run from his wounds and dripped from his wrist. Now he began to groan in terror, the groans gradually turning to shouts.

The pain in his hand was agonizing. Already the slugs had eaten away three of his fingers and now they slithered over the back of his hand, digging deep into muscles and sinew. Harold tugged at the glove, staggering drunkenly around the greenhouse.

He couldn't get it off.

And now his shouts became screams as he wrenched at the glove, still unable to remove it. Blood was now soaking the thick material and his arm was rapidly going numb. Harold felt the bile rising in his throat and he thought he was going to faint, but, if anything, the pain in his hand kept him conscious. White hot agony lanced a path up his whole arm. Again, almost blind with pain and terror, Harold tugged at the recalcitrant glove, screaming even louder when it wouldn't come off.

He groped for the shears, the realization sweeping over him. The terrifying fact of what he must do momentarily numbing even the screaming agony in his hand. He managed to push open the twin blades of the razor sharp shears and, tears rolling down his cheeks, he put his wrist between the twin steel jaws. With his free hand he brought all his weight down on the handle, shrieking with renewed intensity as the blades sliced through the flesh of his wrist. There was a sickening grating sound as they scraped the bone and Harold was splattered with a geyser of his own blood as the veins in his arm were severed. But, despite his frenzied efforts, the shears would not cut through the bone. Skin and muscle tore like fabric, exposing ligaments and twitching sinews and he pounded on the handle like a madman, sweat pouring from his face.

It was then that Jean appeared in the doorway of the greenhouse. She had heard his screams and came running and now the sight which met her caused her stomach to somersault.

She saw her husband pounding madly on the handle of the shears, the twin blades of which closed around his wrist. She saw blood spurting into the warm air, saw the shining white of bone through the pulped and torn crimson mass that had once been flesh and muscle. Blood had sprayed in all directions, onto the dusty worktop, over the glass panels of the greenhouse where it trickled down like sticky crimson rain. Harold's white shirt was covered in it. He was on his knees now, a second away from unconsciousness, the shattered wrist still firmly held in the jaws of the shears and it was at that point she ran to him. Fighting back her sickness, not even able to scream, she watched the glove, moving seemingly with a life of its own as the slugs ate further into his hand.

'The trowel,' gasped Harold, his face purple, eyes bulging like a thyroid sufferer.

Her groping hands found the implement and she stood before him, mesmerised.

'My hand,' he mumbled. 'Cut it off.

She shook her head, her own voice now beginning to rise.

'No,' she said.

'Do it,' he shrieked and his tortured voice spurred her into action. Raising the trowel above her head, she took a last look at the torn and crushed wrist then brought the blade down with terrifying force.

Both of them screamed as the heavy implement scythed through the already shattered wrist. There was a strident snapping of bone and the hand was severed, propelled some distance from the shattered stump by the jets of blood which erupted from the arteries. Harold slumped to the ground, the remnants of his lower arm spouting red geysers into the air. Jean dropped the trowel, blood from the hewn limb splashing her feet and legs.

Harold had passed out.

Jean bolted from the greenhouse, racing back to the house and the phone. Her screams had alerted several neighbours and lights flickered on in the kitchens of the houses next door.

In the greenhouse, the three slugs finished feasting on Harold Morris's severed hand then, leaving only their thick mucoid trails as evidence of their presence, they slithered away.

Eleven

'You know, we should have lived in a bloody flat. Then we wouldn't have had all this trouble,' said Brady, driving his spade into the hard ground.

He turned a few more clods then leant on the spade, the perspiration running freely down his body. He'd removed his shirt even before he started digging and now he felt the unrelenting heat of the sun on his back.

'There's two reasons why you're so worn out,' Kim told him. She was kneeling beside him, pulling weeds from the lawn which was long overdue for a cut. 'You're either out of condition, or...' She looked at him, a mischievous smile on her lips.

'Or what?' he demanded.

'Or you're feeling your age.' She laughed.

Brady picked up a handful of earth and threw it at her. He returned to his digging, determined to prove to her, and to himself, that he wasn't unfit. But, Christ, his body was crying out for a rest. He ached all over and he'd only been out there for an hour. Perhaps Kim was right, perhaps he was out of condition. He slowed his pace a little and looked down at her. She was wearing a pair of dirty old jeans and just her bikini top and he looked admiringly at her deep tan. His own torso was milk white, only coloured in places by the hot sun which had reddened it. Brady didn't tan, he fried. He too wore a pair of old jeans, which hung low at the backside. Together with his big wellingtons, Kim said he looked like a farmer.

Doing the garden was something which Brady had always hated and, in blistering heat such as this, he disliked the task even more. The earth was baked hard, as ungiving as concrete and he had to drive the spade down with all his strength to even break it. But, he struggled on, turning the clods, stopping every now and then to mop his brow with a sodden handkerchief. In the end he gave it up, knotted the white linen square at each corner and pulled it onto his head. Kim looked up and immediately dissolved into fits of laughter.

'You look like Fred Gumby,' she said, referring to the resident idiot of past Monty Python shows. She got to her feet and padded back up the lawn towards the house. 'Fancy a drink?' she called.

He panted exaggeratedly and allowed his tongue to hang over his bottom lip.

'I'll take that as a yes,' said Kim, smiling.

Brady returned to his digging. Inside his thick gardening gloves, his hands felt as if they were on fire but the old spade had a shaft which had grown ragged over the years and he didn't fancy getting splinters, so he struggled on. As he threw himself into his job more, it began to seem less of a battle. Even so, Brady didn't think he could ever acquire a liking for gardening. He and Kim had lain in bed until ten that morning, as was their custom on a Saturday. They had woken at nine and made leisurely love, each seeming more responsive than usual. Brady smiled to himself at the recollection. They would probably just sit out and enjoy the sun when he finished digging. He wondered if he might try his hand at growing some vegetables and he surveyed his expanse of earth like some " feudal baron looking out over his grounds.

It was as he looked down that he saw the first of the slugs slithering onto his spade.

Brady knocked it off, pushing the creature aside with the shovel but it was then that he noticed just how big the bloody thing was. He watched as it slithered away leaving its slime trail behind.

'Good God,' muttered Brady, watching the silvery trail glistening in the sunlight. His mind began to race. Ron Bell's house. The house in Elm Drive. The sewer pipe and now here, in his own garden. He knelt, watching the vile creature closely.

Then he saw another one, as black as night and, Brady guessed, a good six inches long. He swallowed hard, feeling the urge to squash the revolting creatures beneath his spade but he could do nothing but watch in fascinated distaste as the two slugs crawled over the rough ground.

He looked back at the ground he'd already dug. There were more of them. In the six or seven yards of ground which he'd overturned, the Health Inspector counted at least a dozen of the black beasts.

'Percy Thrower, your drink's here,' called Kim, seating herself in a deckchair and sipping her own glass of Bacardi and coke.

Brad ignored her, his eyes still riveted to the slugs.

'Mike,' she called again, noticing that something had caught his attention.

'Come and look at this,' he said, without taking his eyes off the slugs nearest to him. The first one had once more slithered on to his spade and, this time, Brady watched it as it crawled up the smooth metal.

Kim joined him, the glass still in her hand. She caught sight of the slug and shuddered.

'Oh God, what the hell are they?' she said, moving behind her husband as if for protection.

'They're slugs,' said Brady, still watching the crawling monstrosity.

Kim laughed nervously. 'But slugs are small.' She felt the disgust rising within her. 'These are too big.'

The Health Inspector was adamant. 'They're slugs.'

The one on the spade had almost reached the shaft now and Kim watched it with revulsion, her eyes darting over the ground in front of her which seemed to be alive with the black creatures.

'Kill it, Mike,' she urged, watching the beast slithering up the wood but Brady merely reached out and plucked the thing up, holding it between the thumb and forefinger of his thick gloves. It writhed slowly between the digits and reminded the Health Inspector of a fat snake. Its eye stalks swayed as if in slow motion and its mouth moved soundlessly giving the man a glimpse of its many-toothed maw.

'For God's sake, Mike,' Kim persisted. 'Kill the bloody thing.'

Suddenly the slug seemed to twist in Brady's grip, its slime making it difficult to hold, and, before the Health Inspector could react it had driven its vicious sickle shaped tooth into the tough material of his glove.

'Jesus Christ,' he yelped, the sudden attack startling him. Kim put a hand to her mouth to stifle a scream as she watched her husband pull the glove free and throw it to the floor. The slug remained anchored by the tooth, not losing its grip even when Brady hurled it to the ground. Almost with relish he stamped on the hideous black thing, its body making a loud squish as it was crushed. The noise made Kim want to cover her ears, reminding her, as it did, of diarhoettic excretion. Brady ground the thing into shapeless pulp beneath his boot, using the end of the spade to scrape it off his glove. He pulled the glove back on, examining the hole which the tooth had made.

'The bastard tried to bite me,' he said, incredulously. Another eighth of an inch and it would have tasted flesh and that was enough to make Brady shudder.

'What kind of slug bites a man?' asked Kim, looking at the squashed remains.

'That's what I intend to find out,' said Brady, straightening up. He looked at Kim, seeing the uncertainty in her eyes and his tone softened. 'Go and get me a jar, love,' he told her. 'Anything with a screw top lid.'

She nodded and hurried back up the garden. Inside the house she picked up the money jar. They collected all their copper in it, counting it out when the huge jar was full. But, fortunately, it had only recently been emptied and there was less than thirty pence in there. Kim hurriedly emptied it, allowing it to spill out onto the kitchen table, ignoring the coins which fell to the floor. Then, she ran back to where her husband stood watching the other slugs. She put the jar down on the grass and Brady unscrewed the top. He studied the seething black shapes for long seconds then, quick as lightning, he picked one up and dropped it into the jar. He repeated the procedure with one of the larger ones, careful that the vile thing didn't take a chunk out of his finger. Kim shuddered as she saw the things slithering about on the glass, their bodies gliding on the trail of mucus they secreted. Brady snatched up a third slug and dropped it in with the others then he screwed the lid of the jar on as tightly as he could. For long seconds he watched the obnoxious animals slithering around in their efforts to escape then he crossed to the deckchair where his shirt lay discarded. As he buttoned it up, Kim looked into the jar.

'What are you going to do?' she asked.

'Find out what's happening around here,' he said. 'Come on.'

A little bewildered, Kim slipped her shoes on and followed him out to the car.

Brady fumbled in his pocket for the keys, hastily unlocking the driver and passenger doors. They both slid in, Kim yelping in pain when her exposed back came into contact with the blistering hot plastic of the seat. Brady handed her the jar of slugs which she held rather uncertainly, then he stuck the key in the ignition and started the engine. Neither of them spoke and, even as he drove, the Health Inspector couldn't resist the odd anxious look at the three slugs. Almost as if he feared they would escape their glass prison.

He put his foot down, wondering whether the perspiration on his face was entirely the product of the scorching day.

Twelve

The car park of Merton Museum was empty but for a battered old Volkswagen which lay baking in the sun.

Brady brought the Vauxhall to a halt beside it and both he and Kim got out. She handed him the jar with its monstrous black contents and wiped her hands on her jeans. Together, they approached the small flight of steps which led up to the main entrance of the museum. It was a grey stone building, three storeys high, which had been erected about ten years ago and, from the outside it looked like a block of flats but with fewer windows. The windows that were visible reflected the sun back at the two visitors as they advanced, making it difficult to see inside. A feat made all the more impossible because the venetian blinds were down. There was a small notice board outside telling of forthcoming lectures to be given there, or of special attractions to be found in the building itself but Brady was not interested in those.

Followed by Kim, he strode up the stairs, clutching the jar to him as if it were some priceless artefact he'd just dug up. The doors to the museum were open so the two of them walked straight in.

The ground floor was a natural history gallery and they found themselves faced by hundreds of stuffed birds and small animals. A thousand dead eyes followed their progress. Kim glanced into the glass cabinets. She had been here twice before with classes from the nursery and the place always gave her an odd feeling. It was almost like being in a glass fronted zoo, where all the inhabitants were in a state of permanent suspended animation. The baleful eyes of a Tawny Owl fixed her in a glassy stare and she walked on as if mesmerised by the dead orbs. The silence in the building was almost oppressive but at least it was cooler in here and both of them were glad of the respite from the blistering heat outside. Despite the apparent absence of visitors (something which seemed to be a feature of the place), the museum was freshly dusted and spotlessly clean, the wooden floor in particular so heavily polished Kim could see a distorted reflection of herself in it.

They moved through the ground floor gallery, eventually arriving at a staircase. A sign at the bottom proclaimed:

ART GALLERY
LIVE EXHIBITS
ENQUIRIES

A large white arrow showed the way and the two of them followed its course eventually emerging on a landing. To the right lay a desk on which were piled various postcards and brochures depicting exhibits in the museum. There were also pencils bearing the legend Merton Museum. A black sign told them it was an enquiry desk and another pointing arrow indicated a bell and invited them to ring for attention. Brady promptly pressed the button, looking around impatiently when no one appeared. He pressed it again, keeping his finger on it this time, the high pitched ringing echoing through the silence.

A door behind the desk opened and a young man in his early twenties emerged. He held the remains of a sandwich in his hand and was chewing the rest with difficulty, as if he'd taken too large a bite. He raised a hand in greeting, still unable to speak because of the welter of bread and salad in his mouth. Kim smiled, Brady ran an appraising eye over the youth. He wore a pair of faded jeans, crisply pressed all the same, and a T-shirt with 'Iron Maiden' emblazoned across the front. He finally managed to dispose of his mouthful of sandwich and smiled happily at the waiting couple.

'Good afternoon,' he said. 'Can I help you?'

'I want to speak to whoever's in charge, please,' Brady told him.

'Fire away,' said the youth, smiling.

The Health Inspector looked surprised and the young man saw the hint of disbelief on his face. He smiled.

'I know I don't look like a museum curator,' he said. 'That is what you were going to say, isn't it?'

Brady too smiled. 'As a matter of fact it was.'

'John Foley,' he announced, offering his right hand which Brady shook, introducing himself in his official capacity and Kim who smiled at the young man.

'And you're in charge?' Brady asked, as if anxious for reaffirmation of Foley's words.

'Monarch of all I survey,' he said, smiling. 'What can I do for you?'

Brady indicated the jar. 'Ever seen anything like that?'

Foley bent lower, peering through the glass. He frowned and shook his head as he watched the slugs sliding around in their own slime. 'Where the hell did you find these?' he asked.

Brady told him. 'One of them tried to bite me,' he added, producing the holed garden glove as evidence.

'Christ,' said Foley, picking a piece of ham from his tooth. He opened a flap in the desk and walked through, leading the couple up a short flight of stairs to a room marked: 'Staff Only'.

'Come in here,' he said, holding the door open for his two visitors.

The place was like a small laboratory and Kim wrinkled her nose as the unmistakable odour of formaldehyde assaulted her nostrils. The room was small and very hot until Foley flicked on the twin rotar fans above them. Soon, a cooling breeze began to waft around the room. It contained a table with a stainless steel top, a couple of sinks and, on. the work bench which took up three sides of the laboratory, there stood some empty fish tanks.

Brady set the jar down and looked around. Foley pulled up a stool and peered once more at the large slugs in the glass container.

'Do you run this place on your own?' the Health Inspector wanted to know.

Foley shook his head, taking a pair of plastic gloves and a set of stout tweezers from a drawer beside him. 'No. During the week I have an assistant and a woman comes in to clean up but apart from that, I do the lot. Including the exhibits.' He motioned to a newly finished badger which stood on the work top on the other side of the room. 'And no jokes about mounting and stuffing please,' he said, smiling.

Brady grinned but it faded as he saw Foley slowly unscrew the top of the jar. The young man was watching the slugs intently, still not able to believe their size. One was near the top of the jar and it was this one that he aimed his tweezers at, a little disturbed when he saw that they would not reach across its girth. He discarded them in favour of a longer and larger pair, then, cautiously, he removed the lid and inched the tweezers towards the black monstrosity.

'Be careful,' said Brady, feeling Kim take hold of his arm. They both watched as Foley made sure he had a good grip on the implement, then, with a swift movement, he gripped the slug in the tweezers. It wriggled, contracting its body, immediately exuding more slime which dripped onto the work top. Foley held it firmly in the tweezers and pulled a plastic tray towards him. He carefully deposited the slug onto it and then, noticing that the other two were slithering up to the lip of the jar, he promptly knocked them back in and screwed the lid on once more. He picked up a second pair of tweezers and pulled the slug out to its full length. For the first time, Brady saw that the tray in which he'd put it had a scale on it, like a ruler.

Foley exhaled deeply. 'Five and a half inches,' he said. 'Where did you say you found this?'

Brady repeated his story.

'Is it a slug?' Kim asked.

'Oh yes,' Foley told her. 'It's a slug all right but I'll be damned if I've ever seen one this size before.'

'What kind is it?' Brady asked. 'I mean what species?' Foley shrugged. 'I haven't a clue.'

'I thought you were supposed to be the expert,' the Health Inspector said.

The young naturalist looked at him. 'Mr Brady, you probably know as much about slugs as I do. In fact no one seems to know very much specific about them and I certainly don't know anything about this kind.' He nodded in the direction of the captive slug which was writhing and contracting its body beneath the grip of the tweezers. The mucoid coating seemed to be filling the tray around it.

'What's it doing?' asked Kim, shuddering.

'Well, with ordinary slugs, the secretion of bodily mucus is used as a defence mechanism as well as a means of locomotion,' Foley explained. 'If a bird tried to eat it, for instance, the slug would secrete more slime which would cause the bird to drop it. The mucus contains an irritant.' He paused. 'That's what happens with ordinary slugs, I'm just assuming that the same rules apply to these things.' He peered closer, still keeping a firm grip on the black creature. 'You see, when a slug moves it isn't actually in contact with the surface it's on. I know that sounds illogical but what I mean is, it lays down the mucus as a kind of "carpet" if you like, between *it* and whatever it's travelling on. It's the same with snails. Someone did an experiment with one once, they let it crawl across the edge of a razor blade but it wasn't harmed because the slime acted as a cushion.'

'How do they feed?' asked Brady.

'The mouth is on the bottom,' Foley told him. 'There's three or four rows of teeth which it uses to grind up its food.'

'Which is?' the Health Inspector asked, apprehensively.

Foley shrugged. 'Green-stuff mainly. Lettuces, cabbages. Anything they can find in a garden. They're pests, any gardener will tell you that.'

There was a long pause, the silence finally broken by Brady.

'Do any of them eat meat?' he said, quietly.

Foley laughed, softly. 'Not that I know of. There are one or two species that eat earthworms and other insects but…' He let the sentence trail off, his tone darkening. 'Why do you ask?'

Brady swallowed hard. 'Look, I know this is going to sound crazy but could these slugs,' he motioned to the large creatures in the jar, 'kill a man?'

Both Foley and Kim looked at him, aghast.

The young curator smiled. 'That's hardly likely, Mr Brady'.

The Health Inspector's tone hardened. 'One of them nearly took a chunk out of my bloody finger. Now that's pretty unusual wouldn't you say?'

Foley nodded.

Brady continued.

'So there might be other unusual characteristics about them too.'

'Like being able to kill a man?' There was the tiniest trace of cynicism in the curator's voice.

'Is it possible?' the Health Inspector persisted.

'Even if it were, there would have to be hundreds of them.' The young curator quickly qualified his words. 'All the same I'd say it was,' he paused, struggling to find the word, 'unthinkable.'

Kim looked at her husband as if he were a stranger. 'Why do you need to know that, Mike?' she asked.

The Health Inspector was looking at the slug in the tray, still pinned beneath Foley's tweezers.

'A man was found dead two days ago,' he said, softly. 'Ron Bell. He lived in that big house near the new estate.'

Foley nodded.

Brady continued. 'His body looked as though it had decomposed it was…well it looked as though it had rotted. There was no flesh left on him but there was lots of blood in the room where we found him. Now, for a corpse to be in the state he was in, it would have taken months before that amount of tissue deterioration took place and besides that, there wouldn't have been so much blood.'

Kim paled. Foley wrinkled his brow as he listened.

'But, the thing is, all over the remains and all over the room was that slime.' He pointed to the thick, transparent mucus which the slug was exuding. 'And I've seen it again since then. When I was inspecting some new houses I found slime trails on the floor and walls.' He told them about Mrs Fortune's drains. 'I saw slime trails in the sewer too.'

Foley nodded. 'That makes sense. Slugs prefer a damp environment.'

Brady nodded, distractedly and the curator looked at him, not quite sure how he should react to what he'd just heard.

'What are you trying to say, Mr Brady?' he asked.

'I don't know what I'm trying to say, I'm just telling you what I've seen.' He sucked in a worried breath. 'And now, on top of that, I find dozens of slugs, bigger than anyone has ever seen before, in my garden. When I pick one up, it tries to bite me.'

Foley stroked his chin thoughtfully and watched the slug in the tray, slithering about in its own slime.

'So you think that old man was eaten by these slugs?' he said.

'I think it's a distinct possibility. I want to know what you think,' Brady insisted.

The younger man didn't speak.

'Could these slugs kill a man?' asked the Health Inspector again.

Foley inhaled slowly. 'Like I said, there would have to be hundreds of them.'

Brady pressed him, the vision of Ron Bell's remains burning brightly in his mind's eye. 'I'm asking you for the last time.' His voice had taken on a sharp edge. 'Could they have killed Ron Bell?'

'Yes,' said Foley, flatly, his attention now riveted to the slug. He finally turned to face the couple. 'Look, I'll take a look at these slugs, examine them, run some tests on them, do a bit of research. I'll find out all I can about them.' His tone had darkened. 'Give me a day or two.'

Brady nodded.

'Where can I reach you?' the curator wanted to know.

The Health Inspector pulled a nearby pad towards him and scribbled down their address and phone number, then beneath that he wrote down his office number. Foley scanned it once and nodded.

'I'll be in touch,' he said.

Brady extended his right hand and the young curator shook it.

'Thanks,' said Brady and they turned to leave. Foley watched them, listening as their footsteps receded away down the stairs. He sat there for long moments then turned his attention back to the slug in the tray. It was still slithering about in its own slime and had crawled as far as the lip. The curator knocked it back into the tray but, instead of withdrawing its eye stalks like any other slug or snail, it immediately began its journey to the side of the tray again. Foley glanced across at the jar beside him and saw that the other two slugs were clinging stubbornly to the top of it. It was as if the trio of black creatures were anxious to be together again. He pushed the jar closer to the plastic tray and watched, mesmerised, as the freed slug slithered over the lip and onto the glass of the jar. It crawled up the smooth side until it was level with its companions. The curator shook his head, then, taking his tweezers, he plucked the beast from the side of the jar and dropped it into a beaker. Over this he placed a piece of asbestos, normally used in conjunction with a bunsen burner. Then, he got to his feet and passed through a door on his right.

It led into a part of the museum which boasted 'live exhibits'. He flicked the light switches and the powerful banks of fluorescents burst into life. The naturalist walked swiftly towards the thing he wanted, passing half a dozen fish tanks and a vivarium which contained a grass snake. There was also a large tank housing three or four frogs. But it was the tank at the end of the gallery to which Foley was heading. He paused before it, running a swift eye over the inhabitants.

Pond snails.

A number were feeding on the many plants in the aquarium but a large number were clinging to the glass. Foley looked at them, selecting the largest specimens, one of which was the size of a child's fist. Then carefully, he reached into the murky water and plucked the largest animal from its position on the side of the tank. The creature immediately retracted into its shell as Foley tugged it free but, ignoring the water which ran over his hand, dripping on the polished floor, he turned and made his way back to the laboratory. For some reason, as he deposited the pond snail in the tray vacated by the slug, he felt a thin film of perspiration cover his forehead and he was surprised to find that his hand was shaking when he lifted the lid from the beaker.

He seized the slug in his tweezers and held it for a moment, gripping it at the head end just in case it decided to have a go at him as it had at Brady.

The pond snail had emerged from its shell by now and was slithering slowly about in the bottom of the tray.

Foley gently lowered the slug in beside it. He pulled up a stool and seated himself beside the work top, a pencil gripped in one hand, poised over the pad before him. Quite what he expected to happen he wasn't sure but what did happen both shocked and revolted him.

With almost unnatural speed, the large slug slid across to the pond snail and fastened its jaws firmly into the gastropod's head. The slug held firm, its large central tooth anchoring it to its unfortunate victim. The snail tried to withdraw into its shell but was pinned down by the weight and grip of the slug which set to work on it with the numerous rows of radular teeth. Then with one powerful movement, it tore the snail in half, wrenching its soft body from the confines of the shell.

'My God,' gasped Foley, softly, hastily scribbling notes. He watched in awed revulsion as the slug proceeded to devour the remains of the pond snail.

In fact, so intent was he on watching the scene of slaughter before him, he forgot all about the other two slugs in the jar, one of which had succeeded in slithering over the lip and was in the process of heaving its form over the glass of the exterior.

Foley had forgotten to screw the lid on.

He watched the slug in the tray finish off the snail, shaking his head as he scribbled more notes.

The second black creature was half way down the jar by now, its posterior tentacles waving silently.

The slug in the tray now turned towards the curator and he reached for his tweezers once more, ready to drop it back into the beaker.

The second slug was actually on the implement when he picked it up.

With a shout of fear and surprise, Foley dropped the tweezers, the slug falling to the floor with them. He stepped away from the creature as if it were going to leap at him. A quick glance at the one in the tray told him he was going to be forced to act fast. The first slug was slithering over the lip of the tray, leaving its thick trail behind as it gained a grip on the work top. The second was moving towards him. Foley couldn't believe what was happening.

The slug was actually coming after him.

He knelt, retrieved the tweezers and seized the second slug in a powerful grip. With disgust, he hurled it back into the jar with its companion then he turned to deal with the first of the black monstrosities. This time his lunge with the tweezers was clumsy and he snipped off one of the eye stalks.

The creature immediately contracted, slime oozing from its thick body, dark blood running from the severed tentacle. It remained still for a second then, to Foley's horror, it turned towards the metal implement which hovered over its head. The second eye stalk waved around accusingly until Foley, in a fit of anger, snipped that off too. This time the slug did stop, trying to curl up into a ball to protect itself. The naturalist picked it up in the tweezers and dropped it into the beaker, replacing the asbestos mat in position on top of it. Then, he reached into a nearby drawer and took out some adhesive tape which he used to fasten the mat in place. Satisfied that it was secure he sat back on his stool.

The beaker was small, the air supply limited and Foley estimated that it would take less than an hour before the creature suffocated. He screwed the top securely onto the jar which held the two other slugs then he pulled off his rubber gloves and tossed them onto the work top. He crossed to one of the sinks and washed his hands. He was still shaking slightly and, as he dried his hands, he watched the black creatures sliding about inside their glass prisons. He would wait until the one in the beaker was dead and then run some tests on it, perhaps open it up and see exactly what he was dealing with. He decided to go and check the library, to see what he could find out about slugs in general. He folded the towel and draped it over the rail then he headed for the door but, as he reached it he paused and Brady's words came drifting back to him through a haze of uncertainty.

'Could these slugs kill a man?'

Foley closed the lab door and, after a moment's hesitation, he locked it behind him.

Brady and Kim drove from the museum in silence, Kim in particular was disturbed by what she'd heard. She studied her husband's profile for a moment longer then said, tentatively:

'Mike.'

He glanced at her.

'What you said about Ron Bell being killed by slugs. Do you really believe that's what happened?'

He shrugged. 'I don't know what to believe.'

'What did the police report say?' she wanted to know.

'There's been no police report. They're still waiting for the coroner's verdict.'

She shook her head, almost imperceptibly. 'But slugs don't attack people.'

'That one had a pretty good go at my finger,' he snapped.

He swung the car off the side-road, guiding it towards the town centre and Kim asked him what he was doing.

'There's something I've got to get, he told her, his tone softening slightly as he felt her hand on his thigh. He looked across and managed a thin smile and she realized just how worried he really was. He guided the Vauxhall through the heavy traffic in the centre of town and was lucky to find a parking space in the main street. He switched off the engine and took out the keys.

'Fancy a walk?' he asked her and she nodded, clambering out. The inside of Haworth's Garden Suppliers was hot and sticky and Kim found it difficult to breathe. It was a small shop but its shelves were crammed with every kind of gardening aid and the floor was littered with lawn-mowers, rakes, hoes and all manner of other equipment. Their shoes beat out a hollow tattoo on the wooden floor as they walked in and a high pitched buzzing broke the silence as Brady opened the door. Immediately a little man with greying hair and a thin moustache appeared from behind the counter. He was wearing a grey overall and had a pipe protruding from one corner of his mouth. It had long since gone out but he either hadn't noticed or just hadn't bothered to relight it. He spoke without removing it, the bowl bouncing up and down like a rampant metronome.

'Ted Haworth,' he announced, grinning broadly. 'Welcome to my little emporium, what can I do for you?'

'Slugs,' said Brady. 'I want something to kill them.'

'Well, I didn't think you wanted something to feed them with,' said Haworth, grinning at his own quip. He looked at his two customers waiting for them to smile which they did out of politeness. Kim raised an eyebrow and Brady nodded almost imperceptibly.

Haworth scuttled round to their side of the counter, crossing to the shelves which held all manner of bottles and jars.

'Having trouble with the little buggers are you?' he said, gaily.

'You could say that,' said Brady. 'What's the strongest repellent you've got?'

'Now,' said the little man, pausing momentarily. 'Do you want something to kill them or something to just shift them to some other poor devil's garden?' He laughed again.

'I want something to kill them,' Brady told him.

Haworth nodded and reached for a bottle of brown liquid. He plonked it on the counter. Brady read the label. 'Slug-it'. He nodded. 'Anything else?'

The shop owner produced a green can which had 'Slug Pellets' written on it. He crossed back to his own side of the counter.

'I'll take them both,' said Brady, fumbling in his pocket for some money.

'You really have got problems with them, haven't you?' said Haworth, smiling. He dropped the two items into a bag and handed them to Brady along with his change.

'There's full instructions on each container,' he added. 'I had trouble with the little devils one year. They ate me out of house and home. Ruined my crop of vegetables.' He smiled at Kim who tried to look interested.

Brady turned and headed for the door. 'Thanks for your help,' he said, opening it for Kim to pass through.

'They'll get rid of the little sods,' said Haworth, grinning.

Brady nodded. 'I hope so,' he said, cryptically.

It was late afternoon when they finally got home and clouds of tiny flies hovered around Brady as he scattered slug pellets and poison over the ground. Even as he did so he could see a number of the larger slugs slithering about on the dark earth, apparently oblivious to his efforts but he felt a strange kind of pleasure knowing he was sowing the seeds of death for these black monsters. The slug pellets, according to the instructions on the tin, were consumed by the animals and worked almost immediately. There was something in them which attracted the slugs to them. The poison was intended to kill on contact.

Kim watched him from the back door, the clouds of midges swirling around in the afternoon air like flies round a rotted carcass.

When his task was completed, Brady stood back.

'Right you bastards,' he said. 'Come and get it'. He turned and headed back to the house, telling Kim that he'd check on the results next morning.

As the Health Inspector trudged back up the garden a huge black slug, fully eight inches long, slithered up onto a piece of rock. Its eye stalks moved slowly back and forth, almost mockingly.

As if it were watching Brady.

Thirteen

Kath Green picked up the small watering can and poured some of the clear liquid into the pot where the spider plant was growing. The plant was increasing at a tremendous rate and its leaves draped over the side of the pot like some kind of frozen green overflow. Kath smiled to herself and passed to the next pot where she was nurturing a bizzie-lizzie. It had just started to flower, as had a number of the other plants and a heady aroma filled the air of the outhouse.

Playing contentedly on the tiled floor of the conservatory was Kath's two-year-old daughter, Amanda, who was having difficulty dressing one of her dolls. Finally, when she couldn't get its coat on by conventional means, she pulled the arm off in order to ensure an adequate fit. Satisfied with her efforts, she smiled happily to herself and sat the doll down beside a couple of teddy bears and a bendy model of Kermit the frog. Amanda wiped her hands on her dungarees and clambered to her feet, wandering across towards her mother who was busy watering another of her plants. She tugged on Kath's skirt and the woman looked down.

'What is it, darling?' she asked, running her free hand through the little girl's hair.

'Ice cream,' said Amanda, looking up at her with huge brown eyes.

Kath smiled. Obviously the little girl had heard the distant chimes of the van. It usually came past the house at about three every afternoon and, when she herself heard it, she guessed that it must only be in the next street.

'The man's not here yet,' said Kath and Amanda nodded, dejectedly. 'Mummy go and get you one when the man comes round.' That suggestion seemed to brighten her up and she smiled broadly, her little face beaming. She returned to her waiting toys. Kermit and the others greeted her arrival with silence. Amanda picked up the torn off arm of her doll and set about fastening it back in position, chewing it angrily when it wouldn't fit back into the joint. Kath saw her and turned, wagging a reproachful finger at the child.

'Don't put things in your mouth, darling,' she said, taking the doll and its disjointed arm from her irate daughter. Kath fiddled about with the recalcitrant plastic limb for a moment and then she too gave it up as a bad job. 'We'll see if Daddy can fix it when he comes home,' she said, putting the doll on the shelf where she kept her plant food.

'When Daddy gets home,' Kath repeated her own words to herself, sighing wistfully. Ray Green had been working in Stowfield, about twenty miles away, for the past three days and he was due back that night. It couldn't be too soon for Kath. She missed him terribly, even on such short trips. She had never been very good at making friends and, despite the fact that they had lived on the new estate for the past five years, she still only knew most of its occupants on nodding terms. When Ray was on a job she only had Amanda for company and it was at times like that she was thankful they'd had a child. She'd been through a pretty bad bout of post-natal depression but Ray had helped her through it, showing a tolerance and understanding which she had never dreamed he possessed. They were happy in every respect now. Ray's business was flourishing and Kath was slowly learning to overcome her shyness. She had found interests of her own, the plants being her consuming passion. Ray had built the conservatory himself, an extension linked to the kitchen, afraid that the house was becoming like 'Bloody Kew Gardens'.

She smiled at the recollection and carried on watering. As if sensing something, Amanda got to her feet and wandered across to her once more and, just as Kath was going to ask what was wrong, she heard the familiar tones of the ice cream van outside.

'Mummy,' said the little girl, tugging at Kath's skirt. 'Lolly.'

'All right,' said Kath and put down her watering can. She walked through into the kitchen, retrieved her purse and headed out towards the waiting van.

'The sun was still blazing away and Kath decided that she would have one herself. Why not? At twenty-six and with a figure that would make any woman envious, one ice cream wasn't going to hurt was it? She smiled to herself and got in the queue behind a couple of kids, one of whom was busily inspecting the contents of his left nostril on an index finger. Kath shook her head and smiled.

Amanda jumped up and down delightedly on the tiled floor for a moment before returning to her assembled toys. She sat cross-legged amongst them, telling them that she was going to have an ice cream. She put her hand back to steady herself and it was then that she felt something wet on her fingers. Amanda looked down and saw something glistening in the sunlight. At first she thought it was water but, as she ran her fingers through it, she noticed how thick and sticky it was. Puzzled she raised her hand, the clear liquid clinging to her fingers. Amanda brought her hand closer to her face, sniffing at the fluid, puzzled when it had no smell. She looked down and saw that it led right across the conservatory, like a trail.

Tentatively, she licked some of it from her fingers.

It was tasteless too. She swallowed quickly, wiping the rest on her dungarees. Mummy told her all the time not to put her fingers in her mouth and, if she saw her licking the sticky stuff she would be angry. Amanda ran her tongue round the inside of her mouth. The sticky stuff seemed to put her teeth on edge and she tried to wipe it away on her sleeve but, in a moment or two, she had swallowed the one or two globules and it was gone.

She heard her mother's footsteps as she returned with the ice creams and she jumped up to take hers, forgetting the sticky stuff now.

The single slug which had left the trail slithered, unseen, from the conservatory.

Kath cut Amanda's food for her and watched her as she ate. The little girl finished all her tea within about ten minutes and sat back proudly, displaying an empty plate. Kath ate her own meal, smiling as she saw Amanda rubbing her stomach the way Ray did when he had eaten. She glanced up at the wall clock and saw that the hands had crawled round to six p.m. Another three or four hours and Ray would be home. She felt a warm shudder of anticipation run through her.

She finished her own meal while Amanda scuttled off into the sitting room to watch TV. She'd brought all her toys in from the conservatory and they sat with her before the flickering picture. The multi-coloured hues reflected in their dead, glass eyes. Kath did the washing up, watching the sun slowly wane, spilling its redness into the golden heavens, tinting the clouds crimson. She left the plates to drain and padded into the sitting room. Another hour and she'd have to put Amanda to bed. The child was yawning already. Unusual for her, thought Kath. She was usually full of life and bedtimes were sometimes an impossible struggle. Getting her upstairs was bad enough but keeping her in bed was more often than not impossible. Both Kath and Ray often went through three or four story books before the little imp went off to sleep. But tonight, Amanda was dozing in front of the TV and, when seven o'clock came (traditionally a time of joyful but tiring pandemonium) she was positively insistent on going to bed. In fact, even before Kath had finished slipping on her pyjamas, the little girl had fallen asleep. Kath looked down at her as she lay on the sofa but, she reasoned, the child had been out playing all day. There was good cause for her to be tired. She lifted the sleeping form of her daughter easily and carried her up the stairs to the bedroom which had dancing rabbits on the door.

Kath laid her in bed, pulling the sheets up around her neck. She knelt beside Amanda listening to the low guttural breathing for a second then she leant over and kissed her on the cheek. The child moved slightly but did not wake.

'Goodnight, darling,' whispered Kath and crossed to the door. She stood there for a moment, watching the slow rise and fall of Amanda's chest, then she quietly pulled the door shut and made her way downstairs.

Kath heard the dog barking and looked up from her book. She muttered something to herself and got up, crossing to the big bay window in the sitting room. Outside, just passing the house, Mr Steel from next door was being dragged along the road by his Alsatian. The huge dog was yanking him all over the place and Kath couldn't resist a smile. However, her smile faded as the dog stood still before the house and began barking with renewed ferocity. The blasted thing would wake Amanda, she thought and she turned back to her seat, one ear cocked expectantly, waiting for her daughter to call or to come scampering down the stairs.

But, there was no such movement and Kath settled back into her chair, reaching for the discarded paperback. She flipped it open and tried to read but she couldn't concentrate. The barking of the dog had receded into the distance but the ticking of the sitting room clock seemed to be thunderous. Kath looked across at it and saw that it was nearly eight o'clock. She checked her watch too, as if it were going to hasten Ray on his journey home. She discarded the paperback once more and got up to switch on the TV. Kath punched buttons, trying to find something to hold her attention.

A documentary about nuclear war on one channel. She hurriedly switched over. A black and white film. She sighed and pressed the last button. It was another documentary, this time about rising street crime. Kath hovered before the set where a youth with a mohican style hair-cut was being interviewed:

'Well, the fucking law ain't no bother. Me mate, he done this fucking shop and no coppers showed up so, well, I mean they're bastards ain't they? I…'

Kath winced and switched the set off. She exhaled deeply and returned to her chair where she sat for long moments before deciding to make a cup of tea. At least that would keep her occupied.

It was as she rose that she heard the commotion coming from upstairs. Kath stood still for long seconds, listening to the shouts and screams coming from above then, the breath catching in her throat, she raced towards the stairs, hurrying towards the landing. It was as she reached it she realized the noises were coming from Amanda's room.

Kath pushed open the door, her hand reached frantically for the light switch.

Amanda lay across the bed, her body thrashing frenziedly about, contorting like an eel on a hot skillet. Her head was rolling back and forth at a terrifying rate and, Kath noted with horror, that there was a dark, evil smelling mucus spilling over her lips. As her head shook madly, the foul sputum flew in all directions.

Kath took a step towards the bed, the sightless eyes of a teddy bear pinning her in a glassy stare. Its sewn-on smile almost mocking her.

Amanda was rasping asthmatically, her tongue lolling wolfishly from the side of her mouth, the whites of her eyes gleaming like half-moons as they rolled in their sockets.

'Oh God,' gasped Kath, and reached for her daughter, struggling to hold the squirming child still in her arms. She lifted her daughter to her shoulders, the little body twisting forcefully in her arms. Tears welled up in Kath's eyes as she struggled towards the bedroom door. Her vision blurred as the salty droplets cascaded down her cheeks but she staggered on, the wriggling form of her child clasped tightly to her as the convulsions seemed to grow in intensity. Then, suddenly, with lightning speed, Amanda snaked her head forward and bit deeply into Kath's neck, hanging on like a ferret until her mother pushed her away. Kath was screaming now. She stood motionless for a second, gazing down at the inert body of her daughter, then she staggered as she felt the warm blood jetting from the ragged wound in her neck. She clapped a hand to it and felt the torn flap of skin. The crimson liquid was running down her chest, between the valley of her breasts, staining her blouse and she felt her right arm going numb as the pain seemed to spread through her body. The landing swam before her and she gripped the banister to stop herself falling. She felt her knees buckle but she put out a hand and steadied herself, leaving a bloodied hand-print on the white wallpaper. The mark looked black in the twilight.

'Help me,' she gurgled, the blood flowing freely from the bite. It poured down her outstretched arm and dripped onto the carpet and she felt the sickness sweeping over her. Tears coursed down her cheeks as she turned towards the top of the stairs, the phone at the bottom beckoning her.

In her haste, she missed the first step.

For a second Kath clutched at empty air, then, with a despairing moan, she fell forward. Cartwheeling as she crashed down the stairs. She hurtled to the bottom, leaving a trail of blood behind her, some of which splattered up the walls. She smashed into the phone table at the bottom and the phone itself fell to the ground. Twisted like a broken doll, Kath lay at the foot of the stairs, her tortured mind still clinging to the last shreds of consciousness. The pain which racked her body kept her awake. Even through the agony she felt the blood running from her torn neck and, somewhere in the distance, she heard a car door slam.

Ray Green made his way up the short path to the front door and paused on the step, fumbling for his key. He cursed when he couldn't find it, eventually dropping his tool bag and rummaging in the pocket of his jeans. He finally found it and inserted it in the lock smiling wearily. The job in Stowfield had been a sod. He and his partner had worked their nuts off to get it finished on time and it had been bloody hard work, but the size of the pay cheque eased the weariness somewhat and Ray knew how glad Kath would be to see him.

He pushed open the door and walked in.

Kath practically fell into his arms.

For a second, everything seemed frozen, like a stop-frame in a cine film. Ray opened his mouth to say something as he gazed into the tortured face of his wife. She was as white as milk, the blood matted thickly in her hair and stained into her blouse. He saw the vicious bite, the crimson liquid still pumping from it. The blood spattered walls, the wrecked table, the overturned phone.

And then the film was running again.

'Kath,' he gasped, looking into her reddened eyes. She tried to hold him but her fingers slipped and she slid to the floor at his feet. He dropped to one knee, his mind trying to comprehend the sight before him. She raised one bloodied hand, as if soliciting help and he tore off his jacket, laying it over her.

'Amanda,' Kath, rasped, a sudden spasm of coughing racking her body. The movement caused more of the bright red fluid to spill over her lips but she repeated the word, motioning towards the top of the stairs. He hesitated a second then bounded up to the landing taking the steps two at a time. Passing the blood flecked walls until he was looking down at the body of his daughter, now looking so tiny and helpless. Her eyes and mouth were open, a crimson smudge across her chin and lips. He knelt beside the body, shaking his head. Then, with one quivering hand, he reached out and touched her outstretched limb and the tiny hand seemed lost in his own rough one but he clasped it tightly, tears brimming in his eyes. The child's cheeks were sunken pits, her eyes ringed black. The whites seemed to glow even more brilliantly in the darkness but Ray finally tore his gaze from them and scrambled to his feet. He hurried down the stairs, groping for the phone, dialling three nines. He gripped the receiver tightly in his impatience finally managing to blurt out the word 'Ambulance', almost screaming it down the phone. He gave the address and then dropped the receiver, crawling across to Kath who still lay motionless in the hall.

Ray reached for her hand, large salt tears now spilling down his cheeks.

'Oh God,' he breathed, quietly.

Both mother and child were dead before the ambulance arrived.

Fourteen

Brady was up early that Sunday morning. He slid noiselessly out of bed, checking to make sure that he hadn't woken Kim. She rolled onto her back, one hand flailing across the warm area he had just vacated, but she did not wake.

The Health Inspector hurriedly pulled on a pair of jeans. He looked across at Kim once more and then at the clock which told him it was six fifteen. He pushed his feet into his slippers, pulled on his bath robe and padded out of the bedroom. Quickly but quietly he made his way down the stairs, through the house until he finally reached the back door. He unlocked it and slid the bolts back, shivering slightly as an early morning breeze whistled in through the open door.

Brady peered to his right and left, checking that no one else was around. Although at six fifteen on a Sunday morning that was unlikely. Satisfied that he was alone, he padded out into the back garden, cursing as the early morning dew soaked through his slippers and wet his feet.

'Shit,' he grunted, trying to walk on tip-toe to minimise the effect of the wet grass on his fraying foot wear. He moved across to the freshly dug area of ground, some of the slug pellets still in view, scattered on the top soil where he'd left them the day before. He swallowed hard and ran a hopeful eye over the dark earth. Many of the pellets had gone, consumed by the slugs he hoped but there were no dead animals in sight either. He stepped closer, running a hand over his bristly cheeks.

A black slug, the size of his fist, moved slowly towards him and Brady recoiled in shock and disgust. He backed off, seeing that more of the obscene creatures were slithering about on the earth. Brady watched them for a second, the breath catching in his throat, then he turned and headed for the house. He opened the back door and then hurried inside, quickly locking and bolting it again.

He leant against the closed door and exhaled deeply. On the work top opposite stood the can of slug pellets and the bottle of poison.

Brady shook his head.

For all the effect they'd had, he might as well have put down sugar.

Fifteen

By noon that morning the sun had risen high in the sky and it hung in the cloudless heavens covering everything below it with a blanket of searing heat.

David Watson heard the familiar Glaswegian tones of his neighbour, Wally Mackay, and straightened up. The tall Scot had a spade over his shoulder and he sauntered over towards the wire fence which separated the two gardens.

'Hell of a bloody way to spend a Sunday morning,' said the Scot, leaning on the fence. He jumped back hastily rubbing his forearm and looking daggers at the wire which was scorching hot due to the sun. Watson suppressed a grin and tried to look enthusiastic as Mackay leant on the handle of the spade and started chattering away about the weather, his wife and any other thing which passed through his mind. David Watson loved gardening but he invariably got collared by the Scot and ended up doing nothing. It looked like today was going to be one of those days.

'My bloody old lady sent me out here to dig this lot over,' muttered Mackay, indicating the patch of miniature jungle which constituted his garden. The weeds were knee high in places and were beginning to encroach into Watson's carefully tended plot of ground.

'It is getting a bit overgrown, Wally,' he said, trying to sound tactful, but making a melodramatic effort to pull up one of the unwelcome weeds which had found its way in from the Scotsman's garden.

'Fuck it,' said the Scot, peering over his shoulder in the direction of his house. He could see no sign of his wife so he retained his position and fumbled in his trouser pocket for his tobacco tin. He swiftly rolled one and then offered it to Watson who, equally swiftly, declined. He returned to his own task of spreading some compost on his latest crop of potatoes. He'd begun growing vegetables as a joke to begin with and because his wife, Maureen, had bet him a fiver he couldn't do it. The joke turned out to be useful though and he had a fine crop of spuds, onions, carrots and lettuce to show for his efforts. He still didn't know the first thing about the technicalities of cultivating vegetables but he had been lucky. He'd planted the seeds and the things had grown.

Watson enjoyed the peace and solitude which the garden offered him (when he managed to avoid Mackay that was) and it came as a welcome relief from the hustle and bustle of his every day job. He worked for the computer firm in Merton as a rep and had done for the last seven years. The pay was good, he was proficient at the job and he enjoyed it. His wife was manageress of a small but profitable boutique in the centre of town and they were hoping to move from the new estate soon to buy their own place.

They were childless by choice, both of them preferring to pursue their careers rather than sink into a welter of wet nappies and midnight feeds. Maureen in particular, had never shown a desire or even a liking for children. It was something which Watson found unusual but nevertheless welcome. She, unlike others of her kind, never felt the urge to pick up a young child and hold it or to gurgle unintelligible words to new born babies. At twenty-eight, she was every inch the business woman and the emotion which most women possessed had been replaced, in Maureen, by a ruthless efficiency which Watson himself respected. They were a perfect match, for he too bore that unerringly ambitious streak which at times bordered on obsess ion and had, occasionally, been known to veer into vindictiveness. He was thirty-two and happy and, right now, he'd be a lot happier if Wally Mackay stopped nattering and let him get on with his jobs.

'I heard your place was making more redundant,' said the Scot, spitting out a piece of tobacco.

Watson shook his head. 'Just rumours.'

Mackay shrugged. 'I got the fucking push two weeks ago.'

'You told me,' said Watson. About fifteen bloody times, he thought to himself. 'Have you found anything else yet?'

'Nothing about. You haven't any vacancies at your place have you?' he asked hopefully.

Watson smiled thinly and shook his head. 'Afraid not.' He knelt again and pulled a lettuce from the row before him, holding it up to admire his handiwork.

'Got any of those to spare?' said the Scot, admiring the greenery.

Watson looked at him and smiled again. Good old Wally, always on the earhole. The younger man was about to turn when Mackay began talking about football. Reluctantly, Watson halted and listened politely, nodding every so often as the Scot rambled on, his harsh accent grating like fingernails on a blackboard. He chanced a look at his watch and saw that it was twelve -fifteen.

'Dave.'

The shout made them both turn.

Standing in the doorway was Maureen.

'Telephone for you,' she called.

Watson stifled a sigh of relief and made his way up the garden, clutching the lettuce.

Mackay watched the younger man disappear inside his house then he sucked hard on his fag and drove his spade into the iron hard earth. If only my bloody old lady looked like her, he thought.

Watson hurried into the kitchen and inhaled deeply, the delightful aroma of roast beef meeting his nostrils. He dumped the lettuce on the draining board and headed through to the lounge.

'Who is it on the phone?' he asked.

'No one,' said Maureen, laughing. 'I saw that old Rob Roy next door had got you cornered so I thought I'd rescue you.'

Watson laughed and came back into the kitchen. He took Maureen in his arms and kissed her gently on the forehead.

'You cunning bitch,' he grinned, flicking at her blonde hair with one dirty hand. He pulled her close to him feeling the warmth of her body against his. He cradled her head in his hands and kissed her, his tongue seeking hers eagerly. They remained locked together, her right hand reaching for the growing bulge in his trousers, her own nipples stiffening and pressing against the material of her shirt. He finally broke away, shaking his head.

'Lunch,' he said, smiling.

'To hell with lunch,' she said, prodding him hard with her long nail. She drew a line from the hollow of his throat, through the thick hair on his chest, to his navel. As her hand toyed with the button of his jeans he held it and smiled.

'Can't you wait?' he said, trying to sound stern but, when she shook her head he laughed. They finally pulled away from each other and Watson crossed to the sink to wash his hands. He looked at Maureen as he did. She was dressed only in a yellow shirt and a pair of tight -fitting canvas trousers, worn thin at the knees. Beneath them he knew she wore no briefs. She never wore underwear in the summer. The blonde colour was beginning to grow out of her thick hair and the darker roots were showing. Every time she said that she would let her hair return to its natural chestnut colour but, each time, she weakened and resorted to the dye. He watched her as she ran the lettuce briefly under the tap before returning it to the chopping board where she set about its crisp green leaves with a razor sharp knife. She cut it up hastily, dropping the pieces into the nearby salad bowl with the peppers and other vegetables.

'I had trouble finding a decent lettuce,' he said, indicating the vegetable as she tossed it in the bowl. 'Bloody slugs have been at them.'

'Slugs?' She shuddered.

He nodded. 'There's about a dozen out in the vegetable patch now. Damn things. I'll have to see about putting something down to kill them.'

Maureen set the bowl on the table and crossed to the oven, retrieving the meat. She set it on the table and handed the carving knife to Watson. Quickly and expertly he sliced the succulent joint and, within minutes, they were eating.

'No salad?' said Watson, offering Maureen the bowl after he'd taken his share.

She shook her head, reaching instead for the glass of red wine at her elbow. She raised it in salute and smiled.

'Here's to your success,' she said. 'I hope you get that contract signed tomorrow.'

'You're not the only one,' said Watson and joined her in the toast. He put down his glass once more and continued eating. She saw him wince as he pushed a lump of lettuce into his mouth. He chewed slowly for a second, grimaced and reached hurriedly for his wine.

'Something wrong?' she asked.

He motioned to the salad. 'I think I swallowed something,' he said. 'You did wash that lettuce properly didn't you?'

She raised an eyebrow, questioningly and Watson smiled. He continued eating, still aware of the strange flavour but, another glass of wine soon washed away the peculiar taste.

'Where are you taking them to eat tomorrow?' asked Maureen, running the index finger of one hand around the rim of her glass.

'The City Hotel,' he told her.

'That'll cost you.'

He winked. 'It's on the expense account.' He took a sip of his own wine, his voice turning reflective. 'Besides, this is an important contract. It'll be worth millions in the long run if I can secure it.'

'You're worried about it aren't you?' she said.

He nodded. The contract was a big one and, not only would it mean work for the firm for the next three years it would also bring Watson a sizeable slice of commission and almost certain promotion. Perhaps then, they could actually move out and buy their own house. He had two guests to entertain the following morning, one of them an American, and he didn't want anything to go wrong. Selling was his business and he would need all his powers of persuasion at the forthcoming business lunch. For the first time in his working life, he actually felt nervous. Four Mark-1 Computers and it would take him all his abilities to sell them and secure the contract. He sipped at his wine, pouring some more into Maureen's half empty glass with his free hand.

They ate lunch at a leisurely pace, although Watson left the rest of his salad. The strange taste seemed to have returned almost as if it were sticking to his tongue. He drank more wine in an effort to get rid of it and, even if he'd known about eating half the black slug, there was little he could have done about it.

He patted his stomach appreciatively and smiled at Maureen.

'Beautiful,' he said. 'So was the meal.'

She grinned, stood up and crossed to his chair, seating herself on his lap. She ran her carefully manicured fingers through his hair, squirming pleasurably as his left hand found its way up inside her shirt. He cupped one taut breast, rubbing his thumb across the nipple until it hardened to a firm bud. Then, with the other hand, he expertly undid the buttons until both her breasts were exposed. He bent forward and kissed each nipple in turn.

'What about the washing up?' she said, her face flushed.

He smiled. 'To hell with the washing up.'

They both laughed.

Watson checked his watch as the ten o'clock news came on. It was right to the second. He sat in the semi-darkness of the lounge with only the light from his desk lamp and the multi-coloured flickerings of the TV illuminating the room. They had only just drawn the curtains, shutting out the night but he had been sitting at his desk for more than two hours, going over blue-prints and fact-sheets. He had to be sure that he could answer any question that either of his two customers might put to him the following day. Also, he had to know every minute detail about the workings of the machines so that he could extol their worth to the best of his abilities but, as he sat, gazing at the blue-prints, his mind was not on the job at hand. His stomach felt bloated and he had already loosened his belt but, more disturbingly, he was suffering from what felt like severe flatulence. It had come on suddenly about six that evening and despite the repeated doses of Magnesia, the discomfort had not been relieved. He shifted uncomfortably in his seat, rubbing one hand across his protruding belly.

He had eaten nothing since lunch-time, but, surprisingly enough he didn't feel hungry. All he was aware of was the unrelenting pain in his stomach which sometimes felt like contractions. If he'd been a woman he might have thought he was pregnant. He smiled at his own quip but the smile dissolved into a wince as another spasm of pain hit him.

'Jesus,' he rasped, surprised at its intensity.

Maureen, crouching on the floor before the television looked round.

'What's wrong, Dave?' she asked.

He sat back in his chair. 'My bloody stomach,' he said, irritably.

She looked concerned. 'Hasn't that pain gone yet?'

He shook his head.

She got up and crossed to his desk which occupied one corner of the room. 'Do you think I should call a doctor?' she asked.

Watson grabbed hold of her and pulled her onto his knee, trying to disguise the violent stab of pain which accompanied the movement. It felt as if someone was pulling his intestines out through his navel.

'I don't need a doctor,' he said, trying to catch his breath. 'It's probably just nerves from thinking about tomorrow.'

Maureen smiled thinly, not reassured by his home-grown diagnosis. 'If you're sure.'

He nodded. 'I'm sure.' He kissed her. 'Perhaps an early night would help.'

She touched his cheek which felt hot, the perspiration beaded on it in a thin film. Maureen nodded. 'I think that's a good idea,' she said.

In fifteen minutes they were upstairs.

Watson lay in bed, the sheets pulled back. He looked down at his naked body, studying each outline and contour. Lying flat, his stomach didn't seem to be so distended, indeed, when he stood up to examine it in the wardrobe mirror the bloated appearance it had shown earlier seemed to have gone.

The pain, however, persisted.

He crossed back to the bed and lay down again, glancing across at the bedroom curtains which billowed in the gentle breeze. Both bedside lamps were on but the corners of the room were in shadow. He lay still, his arms behind his head, supporting him. The pain seemed to have moved further up his body and, as he swallowed, a wave of agony seemed to sweep over his entire stomach and lower chest. He cursed silently. Perhaps it *was* just nerves. Maybe something he'd eaten? He nodded, yes, that was the answer. In the morning it would be fine, he'd...

He sat up as an excruciating pain tore through him from sternum to groin. He clutched the bed, the muscles in his arms standing out like cords of thick hemp but, after a few unbearable seconds, the spasm passed, even settling a little. He took a deep but tentative breath and lay back again. He heard the toilet flush and, a second later, Maureen's light footsteps padding across the landing.

She entered the bedroom and closed the door behind her, the long black, diaphanous, night-dress swirling around her like nylon fog. Through it, Watson could see the smooth outline of her body and she stood before him for long seconds gazing down at his own naked form. He shifted his position slightly, gritting his teeth. against the onslaught of pain he expected. It came only briefly and he exhaled gratefully, watching as Maureen climbed into bed beside him.

Her left hand stroked soothingly across his belly.

'Does it feel any better?' she asked.

He nodded and leaned forward to kiss her, feeling that soft hand sliding further down his body until it enveloped his penis, stroking and caressing it until it reached full erection. Watson thrust his hips forward, forcing his shaft further up into Maureen's eager hand. He reached for the bow at her throat and pulled it, allowing the night-dress to fall away, exposing her body. He cupped one breast in his hand, bending his head to flick the rough edge of his tongue over her swollen nipple. She held his free hand, pushing it towards her mound where his fingers brushed the soft down of her pubic hair before plunging deeper to find her slippery cleft. She writhed beneath his probing digits and he pushed deeper, smiling at the look of pleasure on her face.

Her hand gripped his organ more tightly, the speed of her movements increasing and Watson felt the unmistakable waves of early pleasure sweeping over him. He kissed Maureen gently on the lips, whispering to her to slow down but her passion knew no bounds and she pulled him onto her, guiding his hardness into her moist vagina. He thrust into her, both of them gasping at this new ecstasy.

Watson almost cried out in pain as a wave of agony tore through his stomach and chest. He gritted his teeth, sucking in a tortured breath, suddenly finding that his arms would not support him. He collapsed onto Maureen, the pain driving red hot knives into him.

He withdrew from her and rolled to one side, his penis immediately losing its stiffness.

'Dave,' gasped Maureen, breathlessly. 'What is it?'

He winced. 'Jesus.' The word sounded as if it came from miles away. Watson was clutching at his stomach, lying still on his back.

'I'm going to get a doctor,' said Maureen, hauling herself out of bed.

'No,' he said, forcefully. 'It's OK now.' He nodded, noting that the pain was, indeed, diminishing.

Maureen paused, her hand still on the knob of the door but, when she saw him stand up, she crossed back to the bed. Watson stood before the mirror once more. There was no distension, just the pain. He took three or four deep breaths, relaxing more with each one. Finally he returned to bed. Maureen lay beside him, stroking his hot cheek with one index finger. He twisted his head to one side and kissed her finger, smiling at her.

'Are you going to be all right?' she said, anxiously.

Watson nodded. 'The pain's almost gone now.' He smiled. 'I'll be as right as rain in the morning.'

They switched off the bedside lamps and Maureen drew herself closer to him. It wasn't long before he heard the soft, rhythmic sound of her breathing as she drifted off to sleep. Watson watched the curtains, still billowing in the gentle breeze. Beyond them the night was black, sticky with heat.

The pain gradually lessened in David Watson's stomach but, the hands of the clock had crawled round to one twenty a.m. before he finally found the welcome oblivion of sleep.

It was Maureen who heard the alarm the following morning. She reached up and turned it off, simultaneously touching Watson gently on the shoulder.

'Dave,' she murmured, her voice thick with sleep.

He didn't move.

She called his name again, rubbing her eyes and blinking myopically at the ceiling.

Still no response.

Maureen propped herself up on one elbow and leant across her husband. He was lying on his side with his back to her and, when he made no movement on her third call, she shook him gently.

Watson remained still.

Maureen swallowed hard and swung herself out of bed, crossing to her husband's side where she knelt. She pressed a hand to his cheek which was cool and suddenly she felt afraid.

'Dave,' she repeated, more urgently, this time shaking him hard.

She gave an audible sigh of relief when he opened his eyes a fraction. Crusted and heavy-lidded, they opened slowly and he looked at her almost as if she wasn't there. He seemed to be looking through her.

Maureen called his name again and, this time, he rolled onto his back. His mouth opened slightly and he made a deep rasping noise in the back of his throat.

'God Almighty,' he moaned, covering both eyes with his hands.

'I thought you were dead,' she said, her breath coming in short gasps.

'I think I am,' croaked Watson, massaging the bridge of his nose between his thumb and forefinger. 'It feels like there's a brass band marching around inside my head.'

'What about your stomach?' she wanted to know.

He sat up slowly, the headache intensifying to a point where he felt as though someone were hitting him repeatedly across the skull with a dozen red hot hammers. He slumped against the headboard and looked down at his stomach. No distention. No pain even. With cautious hands, he pressed the firm flesh in several places.

'No pain at all,' he said, trying to smile but the blinding white agony in his head restrained him. 'It's my bloody head now.'

'I'll go and get breakfast ready. I'll get you a couple of Paracetamols,' Maureen said and pulled on her house-coat. She padded out of the bedroom leaving Watson alone. As slowly as he could he swung himself out of bed and crossed to the bedroom door. The headache seemed to intensify as he walked across the landing to the bathroom and, when he looked at his reflection in the mirror, a haggard, white-faced ghost stared back at him. His face was the colour of rancid butter, the dark circles beneath his eyes looking all the more prominent because of that. He ran some cold water and splashed it over his face, leaning over the sink for what seemed like an eternity. When he did finally straighten up, he put both hands to his temples as if he were afraid his head was going to explode. With the red hot hammers pounding away at his brain, he began to remove his shaving equipment from the glass-fronted cabinet on the wall. He filled the sink with hot water and, carefully, lathered his face.

The prospect of a day's business and hard selling seemed to make his pain all the worse.

Sixteen

The dining room of the City Hotel was already crowded with its daily quota of businessmen as Watson and his two customers entered. He'd booked a table for one fifteen and a quick glance at his watch told him that it was over thirty minutes before they were due to eat.

'How about a drink before lunch?' he said, smiling, trying to ignore the headache which still raged, threatening to split his skull in two.

'Sounds good to me,' said Edward Canning, the first of his prospective customers. Canning's thick American drawl drifted through the air, mingling with the smell of cigarettes, liquor and the tempting aroma of freshly cooked food. Canning was in his late thirties, heavily built but without a hint of fat on his powerful body. He lit up one of his huge cigars and followed Watson and the other man, Kenneth Riggs, into the smaller of the City's three bars.

Riggs was younger by a couple of years but his grey hair gave him the appearance of someone twice his age. His face was lined and his cheeks seemed to hang down like those of a bloodhound. When he laughed, which he often did, a row of double chins wobbled fluidly, spilling over onto his shirt collar which looked so tight it threatened to strangle him. Canning had removed his tie because of the heat and, as he found a table near the window, he rolled up his sleeves. Riggs joined him while Watson stood at the crowded bar brandishing a five-pound note in front of him.

He looked angrily at a man who bumped into him and the unfortunate chap apologised hurriedly when he saw the

112

expression on Watson's face. His nerves were not so much frayed as shredded. He'd picked his two customers up at nine and driven them to the factory to show them the computers in action. They had asked surprisingly few questions, only those relating to reliability, performance, output and, most importantly, cost. A fact for which Watson was grateful because he was finding it difficult to even think straight, so intense was the throbbing inside his skull. Nevertheless, he'd established a good rapport with the two men, particularly Canning. Both seemed interested and satisfied with his approach and also the computers. Watson felt almost certain that the contract would be signed but he would feel a hell of a lot happier when he could actually see their names on that dotted line. He exhaled deeply, closing his eyes momentarily. The noise in the bar seemed to swirl around him like a bank of mist yet it seemed distant, as if he were alone in a sealed compartment and everyone else was outside. He opened his eyes again, craning forward to see where the barman had got to. The little man in the red jacket was serving a couple of customers at the far end of the bar so Watson continued to stand in his place holding up the fiver as if hoping it would attract the barman. He ran one hand across his forehead, wondering if his headache was ever going to go. The two tablets he'd taken at breakfast had done nothing to help, neither had the four others he'd taken since. He just hoped that the deal could be concluded quickly. He promised himself he'd go straight home to bed afterwards.

The barman finally arrived and Watson ordered, leaning against the counter while the little man fetched the drinks. He returned with surprising speed and Watson collected both drinks and change and made his way carefully across the room to the table where his customers sat.

He almost fell into the seat, reaching for his vodka.

'Cheers,' he said, his false smile returning with effort.

The other two men echoed his toast and there was a moment's silence as they drank.

'What do you think of the place?' asked Watson, finally.

Canning scanned the bar and the dining room beyond. The walls were festooned with a mixture of rusty farming implements and old weapons. In the next, larger, bar, there was a huge open fireplace stacked high with logs over which hung a full size man-trap.

'Big mice around here, huh?' said the American, smiling.

Riggs laughed loudly, spilling some of his drink.

'They used to use them for catching poachers,' Watson told his customer.

The man-trap was about the only authentic piece of apparatus in the entire hotel. It was what some people might call a 'plastic restaurant'. The wooden beams which criss-crossed the ceiling were imitation and even the massive log fire was lit by a gas flame hidden beneath the wood. The weapons and prints were antique shop acquisitions designed to give the place a feeling of age and character which was palpably second hand. Two suits of rusty armour stood guard at either side of the fireplace, as if guarding the secret of its falseness.

The dining room itself was festooned with flags bearing the emblems of dukes and lords who had probably never existed and a stag's head hung from the central wall. Canning saw it and touched Watson on the arm.

'I was just thinking,' said the American, a wry smile on his lips. 'That goddam deer must have been doing about ninety when it hit the other side of that wall.'

Watson laughed his polite laugh and Riggs once more went into a fit of giggles, spilling more of his drink.

'Is your boss expecting us to sign a contract today?' asked Canning, sipping at his drink.

Watson shrugged. 'Well, he's not banking on it, but it'd be a nice surprise for him.'

The American smiled.

'And a nice bonus for you.'

Watson nodded, the movement sending fresh jabs of pain through his head. He gritted his teeth and smiled, downing what was left in his glass.

'You are prepared to guarantee us full maintenance, free of charge for the next five years if we accept the deal?' said Riggs, studying the salesman over the rim of his glass.

'Yes,' said Watson.

Riggs nodded. 'So, the only thing that still is to be worked out is the price.'

'The price was agreed, Mr Riggs,' said Watson. 'There's no machine comparable to the Mark-1. You'll find nothing better for your particular needs, not at the prices we're offering anyway.' He paused, seeing that he had both men's eyes on him. 'In the long run it will be an investment. You *could* buy cheaper elsewhere, I wouldn't attempt to delude you about that. But nowhere will you find a machine with the capabilities which ours can offer.'

'How long have you been doing this job?' asked Canning, a slight grin on his face.

'Seven years,' Watson told him, slightly puzzled.

The two customers exchanged an enigmatic smile which unsettled the rep slightly.

'You're very good at it,' Riggs told him.

Watson thanked the man, wishing that he'd just put his bloody name on the contract instead of lavishing compliments on him. Riggs asked a few more questions about the computers which Watson answered with his usual thoroughness. The grey haired man nodded but didn't speak. There was an awkward silence between the trio which was finally broken when a nasal sound came over the small speaker in the bar. The garbled tones chattered on for a moment and Watson finally made out the sound.

'Mr Watson,' said the voice. 'Your table for three is now ready. Mr Watson.'

The three men got to their feet, a wave of pain so powerful it staggered him, causing the rep to support himself against the wall for a second. His head felt as if it were going to split in half and he had a mental picture of his brain swelling, trying to burst free of the confines of his skull. He stood still for a moment, his fixed smile finally fading.

Canning saw him swaying slightly and put out a hand, as if fearing that the younger man were going to fall.

'You OK?' asked the American.

Watson sucked in a laboured breath. 'Yes, just a bit of a headache.' He found the smile once more and looked at the two men. 'You carry on into the dining room. I'm just going to the toilet.'

Canning hesitated but the salesman raised a hand to signal that he was all right. He watched the men walk into the dining room then he made his way to the lavatories.

The cold white light which flooded from the banks of fluorescents made him wince and his feet echoed on the white tiled floor. He found that he was alone and crossed to the nearest sink, fumbling in his jacket pocket for the jar of Paracetamol. He unscrewed the cap and scooped a handful of running water to swallow the pills with. They remained on his tongue for brief seconds, the bitter taste making him feel sick but then he swallowed them, clutching the side of the wash basin. He groaned aloud as the pain in his head pounded away. It seemed as if the red hot hammers had been replaced by hundreds of blazing chisels and someone was driving them relentlessly into his tortured brain. He bent and splashed his face with cold water, straightening up slowly to gaze at his pain racked features in the mirror.

A single drop of blood trickled from his left nostril. It ran slowly down and over his lip, falling to the sink beneath where it made a tiny crimson explosion on the white enamel.

Watson shuddered and wiped it away with the back of his hand. He washed his hands hurriedly and dried them on the nearby towel-roll then he returned to the mirror.

There was no more blood and he dabbed at the nostril with his handkerchief, relieved to find that it showed no hint of red when he inspected it. He swallowed hard, steadied himself against the basin edge then walked out.

He saw Canning and Riggs seated at a table in the centre of the dining room, talking animatedly, only slowing their machinations when they saw him approaching. He smiled and sat down, draping the napkin across his knees.

'Feel any better?' the American asked.

'Yes, thank you,' Watson lied, reaching for the menu which lay before him. The waitress was approaching, order pad at the ready and Watson had only seconds to skim the menu before ordering. The waitress took the order, (steak for Watson and Canning, Spaghetti Bolognese for Riggs) and was about to walk away when the rep added a postscript.

'And a bottle of the Beaujolais please.'

The waitress nodded and disappeared.

'Well Mr Watson,' said Canning, stroking his chin thoughtfully. 'While you were elsewhere, my partner and myself made a decision.'

Watson swallowed hard, trying to forget the blinding headache for a moment.

'We'll accept the terms of your contract,' the American told him, flashing him a mouthful of capped teeth. He extended a hand which Watson shook thankfully. Riggs too repeated the gesture.

'I thought we might finalise things and sign over a drink after lunch,' said Riggs, smiling.

'Thank you,' said Watson, one hand almost unconsciously touching his nostril. He looked at the hand, relieved when he saw that it bore no crimson mark. His head was still thumping and the noise created by the many other diners made him dizzy but, the realization that he'd secured the contract was at least one worry less.

The waitress returned with the wine, uncorked it and poured some into Watson's glass. He sipped and nodded. She put it down and left them. The rep filled the other men's glasses and they raised them in salute.

'I suppose this ought to have been done with champagne really,' he said, smiling.

'What the hell,' Canning said, grinning. 'A drink's a drink. Here's to our agreement.'

They drank. The waitress returned a moment later with the food which she put down before the three men. They began eating, their conversation now veering away from business. Canning started talking about his family but the words didn't seem to register with Watson who had put down his knife and fork and was sitting motionless in his seat, his fists clenched so tightly the knuckles were white. He found it difficult to breathe and, when he tried to swallow it was almost impossible.

Canning looked up and saw him.

'Hey,' he said, a sense of urgency in his voice. 'What in the hell is wrong, David?'

Watson reached for his wine and raised it to his lips.

'I told you,' he said, his voice a dry rasp. 'It's this bloody headache.'

He managed to get a couple of mouthfuls of wine down, almost slamming the glass back onto the table. He reached for his knife and fork again and cut his steak, the pain, unbelievably, intensifying.

Riggs, peering up from his plate of spaghetti bolognese, was the first to see it.

A thin, almost watery, trickle of blood ran from Watson' s nostril and dripped onto the table cloth. It left little stain but then, suddenly, it began to thicken and grow darker and within seconds, viscous clots were gushing from the nostril. They splattered onto the tablecloth and even onto Watson's plate with a force and sound which made Riggs feel sick. The rep put a hand to his face and groaned, the blood spilling through his fingers and running down the back of his hand. He remained upright in his seat, clutching at the nostril which was pouring forth blood like a tap with no washer.

'Jesus H Christ!' murmured Canning, pushing himself back and away from the table.

And now other diners had seen or heard the commotion and all eyes turned towards the horrendous scene.

Watson rocked back and forth in his seat, hands clapped to his head as the pain reached intensities beyond endurance. Blood continued to gush from his nostril and then, to the horror of all those watching, something white appeared amidst the welter of crimson. Something long and tapering which seemed to grow from the very nostril itself.

'Oh my God,' gasped Riggs.

The worm wriggled free of the nostril, its white body covered with blood. Then, as it tore its obscene form from the bursting orifice, Watson shrieked and pitched forward. He crashed into the table, plates, glasses and food cascading down after him as he grabbed at the tablecloth, which fell across him like a blood-spattered sheet. He rolled onto his back, the worm slipping down his cheek. It lay in the pool of crimson beside him.

A waitress nearby screamed and dropped an armful of plates, people began to bump into each other in their efforts to get away from the abominations before them. Only Canning remained nearby, transfixed by the sight. Watson's body was twitching madly, the muscles going into spasm so quickly he looked as if someone were tugging him about with invisible wires. Then, as the American watched, the flesh of Watson's eyelid seemed to split, as if someone had pulled it too hard. There was a small jet of clear liquid, some of which spurted onto Canning's leg and then, the eye began to bleed. The white turned crimson, the blood vessels appearing to swell and then burst.

A second white shape came writhing up from the rent in the eyeball.

The second worm was bigger and, when it finally succeeded in tearing its vile form free, Watson's eye collapsed in on itself. Blood pumped thickly from the ruined socket.

The worm slid across his face, touching the fluttering lips briefly and, with a newly awakened disgust, Canning thought that the monstrous thing was going inside his mouth but it lay there for a second then seemed to stiffen and it rolled off into the puddle of blood along with the first creature.

Watson raised one blood spattered hand as if soliciting help and his remaining eye fixed Canning in a baleful stare, then, the hand fell away and the American could see that the younger man was dead. His face a bloodied ruin, he lay amidst the spilled food and the gouts of his own blood.

Riggs had passed out.

A waiter appeared at the American's side and looked down at the body. He swiftly turned his head, fighting back the hot bile which was clawing its way up from his stomach.

'Fucking hell,' he groaned.

'Get an ambulance,' said Canning, kneeling to help Riggs up.

The dining room was filled with noise. Somewhere a woman was crying somebody was shouting something about it being an accident. The waiter was phoning for an ambulance.

That done, he hurriedly dialled the Council Offices and asked for the local Health Inspector.

Canning took one last look at the body of David Watson, his own stomach doing somersaults but it wasn't the appearance of the body which drew his attention. It was the two white shapes which lay beside it and, finally, he lost control and retched until there was nothing left in his stomach.

Seventeen

Brady pulled up outside the City Hotel and was surprised to see up to a dozen people standing on the steps which led up to the main doorway. He locked the Vauxhall and strode across, pushing through the group into the lobby. There was no sign of any ambulance or the police and the Health Inspector wondered just what the hell was going on. He'd received the call about ten minutes ago and come straight out. Some garbled message about an accident at the Hotel, could be hygiene problems and then the caller had hung up.

The Health Inspector made his way through the group of people on the steps and walked through the lobby, his feet sinking into the deep pile of the crimson carpet. He frowned. There were more people huddled about outside the entrance to the dining room. A woman was sitting in a chair nearby and, as far as Brady could ascertain, someone was waving smelling salts under her nose.

He pushed open the door of the dining room and found several red shirted waiters standing around, all looking into the area where the tables were. There were two or three men in suits there as well and it was one of these who approached the Health Inspector. He held up his hands, as if to bar Brady's way.

'Sorry, sir,' he said. 'No one is allowed into the dining room. If you'd just like to wait...'

Brady cut him short. 'I'm the Health Inspector,' he said, producing a small plastic ID card which bore a very old and poorly taken photo of him.

The man looked at the card then at Brady, as if the likeness didn't fit but he handed it back, regarding the official suspiciously.

'What are you doing here?' the man wanted to know.

Brady snatched the card back, irritably.

'It's why I'm here, you should be worrying about,' he rasped. 'Now, what happened?'

'There was an accident in the dining room,' said the man. 'We're not really sure what it was.'

Brady regarded the man indifferently. 'Are you the manager?'

He shook his head. 'He's away for the day. I'm the assistant manager, anything you...'

The Health Inspector cut him short again. 'Can I see your...' he paused, '...accident?'

The man in the suit snapped his fingers towards a young waiter who Brady guessed must be in his early twenties. The lad looked round.

'Show this gentleman to the...er... the body,' he said.

'Why can't you show me?' asked Brady.

The man blenched and swallowed hard. 'Robinson will show you.'

The Health Inspector smiled to himself and followed the young waiter. As he walked past tables he noticed that most of them bore plates of food; some still steaming. The aroma reminded him that he hadn't had lunch.

'There,' said Robinson, pointing to a blood-stained cloth. Beneath it lay the body of David Watson.

Brady knelt and lifted one corner of the tablecloth.

'My God,' he whispered, pulling the cloth back further to reveal the upper torso as well as the face. He looked at the corpse, the blood now thickly congealed on it, the ruptured eye socket looking as if someone had filled it with rancid crimson syrup. Watson's other eye was open. It reminded Brady of Ron Bell's head with its single staring eye.

'Who called the ambulance?' Brady said, swallowing hard.

'I did,' the waiter told him.

Brady looked up at the youth. 'Was it you who called my office?'

Robinson nodded.

It was then that Brady noticed the worms.

He took an involuntary step back and nearly overbalanced, the tablecloth falling from his grasp and uncovering the body. For long seconds he remained crouching, looking at the motionless forms of the worms both lying in the congealed gore, then he moved closer. He estimated that the worms must be around seven or eight inches long, but, unlike ring-worm they were not segmented. Just long white threads about as thick as two spaghetti strands.

'Was that why you called my office?' asked the Health Inspector, glancing over his shoulder. The group of waiters and the three men in suits were out of earshot but, nevertheless, the older man kept his voice low.

Robinson nodded. 'I thought those… worms might have come from the food.' He paled. 'I mean, the fucking things came out of his eye.'

Brady reached for a knife which lay on the floor nearby. With it, he carefully lifted one of the worms into the air, making sure he kept it at arm's length. The limp body hung there without moving.

'It seems dead enough,' he said, quietly.

'What is it?' Robinson asked, revolted by the sight of the foul thing. A jellied blob of coagulated gore dripped from one end of it and narrowly missed splashing Brady's trousers.

'Give me a glass or something,' he said. 'Anything I can put them in.'

The young waiter turned and saw an empty pint glass, he snatched it up and handed it to the Health Inspector who hurriedly dropped the first worm into the bottom. Then, he scooped the second creature up out of the puddle of congealed blood and deposited that in the glass as well. The task completed, he dropped the knife, draped a serviette over the top of the glass and hurriedly fastened it to the lip with an elastic band from his pocket.

He held the glass up, studying the blood-flecked white forms inside.

It was as he was straightening up that he caught sight of two ambulance men pushing through the dining room doors. One was carrying a furled stretcher, the second a red blanket. The latter of the two recognised Brady and nodded affably, then he looked down at the body of Watson.

'What happened to him?' said the ambulance man, holding the blanket while his companion unrolled the canvas stretcher beside the corpse.

Brady shook his head slowly, holding the glass and its vile contents down by his side. He watched as the two men lifted Watson onto the stretcher. The red blanket was draped over him and they lifted the body. The Health Inspector walked behind them, keeping the glass by his side but the people outside were more interested in the shape on the stretcher and he pushed through the crowd unnoticed. A couple of police cars, their blue lights turning silently, had just pulled up across the street and Brady saw three or four uniformed men crossing towards the ambulance. He, himself, reached his car and propped the glass up on the passenger seat. He sat still for long moments, his eyes fixed on the monstrous creatures inside and he was thankful that they were dead. Now he had to find out just what they were.

He twisted the key in the ignition and the Vauxhall engine burst into life. He drove off, for some reason, feeling the need to look at the worms every so often. The glass rocked on the seat and, once, toppled over. Brady hastily stood it up again.

He drove quickly and, this time, he knew that the perspiration which stained his forehead wasn't caused by the heat.

He brought the Vauxhall to a halt in the museum car park next to Foley's battered Volkswagen. There were a couple of other cars parked there as well and a bus with 'MERTON JUNIOR SCHOOL' emblazoned on the side.

The Health Inspector snatched up the glass, locked his door and sprinted up the short flight of steps to the main door. He entered the lower gallery and was immediately surrounded by a group of kids about ten or eleven years old. They swarmed round the gallery, note-pads in hand, scrawling down the names of the exhibits while a bespectacled woman in her forties called out to them to make sure they wrote down every name. The kids babbled excitedly, one or two banging into the Health Inspector who finally fought his way through the throng and reached the stairs. He hurried up them to the enquiries desk and rang the bell, looking around impatiently when no one came. Once more he rang the bell and still no one appeared so he turned and took the three or four steps which led to the laboratory. He knocked and a familiar voice told him to wait.

A moment later, the door opened and Foley stood there. The young curator smiled broadly and ushered Brady inside.

'How's it going?' he said, wiping his wet hands on his jeans.

Brady held up the glass. 'You tell me. '

The younger man took it from him and set it down on the work top, carefully removing the makeshift cover. He reached for a specimen tray and tipped the worms into it, prodding them with the tip of a scalpel.

'Where did you get these?' he asked, his voice heavy with foreboding.

Brady caught the note of concern in the curator's voice and stepped closer.

'A man just died in the City Hotel,' he said. 'One of the waiters called me, he thought these worms might have come from the food.' Brady paused, sucking in a laboured breath. 'He said he saw one of them come out of the bloke's eye. Now what the hell do you make of that?'

Foley didn't speak, he just leant closer to the dead worms, noticing, as Brady had, that they were unsegmented.

'Well,' the Health Inspector persisted. 'That's impossible isn't it?' The question hung heavily in the air. 'I've seen ring worm, other parasites, dozens of times but never anything like this. Foley, for Christ's sake. It's not possible is it?'

The naturalist turned round to face Brady.

'Those slugs you brought in the other day,' he said. 'I ran some tests on them.'

Brady interrupted, irritably. 'All right, we'll talk about the slugs in a minute. I need to know about these bloody things.' He pointed at the worms.

'That's the whole point,' said Foley, raising his voice slightly. 'The slugs and these worms are linked.'

'How for God's sake?' asked the Health Inspector, sitting down on a stool nearby.

'After you left that day, I dissected one. I found out everything I could about it. I read as many books as I could find about the bloody things.'

'And?'

Foley exhaled deeply. 'Well, for one thing, they're not a new species. As far as I can tell they must be a kind of hybrid.'

'What makes you so sure?' Brady wanted to know.

'Because they're ordinary garden slugs,' said Foley, flatly.

Brady almost laughed. 'Foley, the damn things are eight inches long. That one you measured was five and a half inches and that was a small one. Now, anybody will tell you that a common black slug is about three-quarters of an inch long and what's more, they don't usually bite.'

'That's what I meant about them being hybrids,' the curator explained. 'They must have inter-bred with another species. There are three species of carnivorous slug in this country. Testacella maugei. Testacella haliotidea and Testacella scutulum. Now those three hunt and kill earthworms and other insects, sometimes other slugs.'

Brady interrupted him. 'Then they wouldn't mate with garden slugs, they'd eat them.' He paused. 'Besides, you said that these large slugs were the ordinary garden variety.'

'They certainly share all the same physical characteristics apart from the fact that they seem to eat meat,' said the curator.

The Health Inspector exhaled deeply.

'I just haven't got a clue why or how ordinary garden slugs could grow to sizes like we've seen, or why they should have become carnivorous;' said Foley, wearily. 'My theory about inter-breeding is all we've got. '

'But slugs are hermaphrodite aren't they?'

Foley nodded. 'But they rely mainly on ordinary mating to reproduce. That just compounds our problems. They can cross-fertilize and fertilize their own eggs.'

There was a long pause the silence finally broken by Foley.

'It might interest you to know that each female can lay up to one and a half million eggs a year.' He reached for his coffee and took a sip, wincing when he found that it was stone cold.

Brady didn't speak.

Foley tried to qualify his statement. 'There's a tremendously high mortality rate. These slugs seem to be cannibals too, the younger ones are eaten by the larger animals in the clutch. Out of a hundred eggs laid, only three or four slugs will actually reach full maturity. Even so, when each female can lay one and a half million eggs a year, that's still a hell of a lot of slugs. The only thing is, they must have damp conditions to lay them. '

The Health Inspector nodded. 'Like the sewers,' he whispered to himself.

'I also found out that the irritant in the slime trails of these particular slugs is lethal,' said the curator.

'How?'

'I gave some to a laboratory rat. The damn thing was dead in three hours. Now, working on that example I'd say that the slime would be fatal if consumed by, say a child for instance. What it would do to an adult I couldn't say.'

'How would it affect a child?' Brady wanted to know.

'Well, judging by the symptoms which the rat manifested,' he paused, momentarily. 'I'd say the victim would appear almost rabid. They'd probably undergo convulsions, mental disturbance. The rat turned savage, it killed the female that was in the cage with it.'

Brady wiped a hand across his forehead. 'I can't believe this,' he said, incredulously.

Foley nodded. 'I wish it wasn't true.'

'How do they move around?'

'Crawl. Burrow. Swim. Lots of ways.'

'So they could be using the sewers to move around in?' said Brady, although it sounded more like a statement than a question.

'Without a doubt,' said the curator. 'Anywhere there's plenty of moisture, and it would suit their egg laying habits.'

'But if they need moisture, how come there's so many of them about now? It's hotter out there than it has been for years.'

'These particular slugs have a very large mucus gland. They secrete huge amounts of slime so there's no danger of them "drying up" even in the hottest weather. That's what makes them so much more dangerous, they're not reliant on a damp environment. Although we're more likely to find them in one, they don't *need* it like ordinary slugs do.'

'My God,' groaned Brady.

'I don't know how long these slugs have been breeding,' said Foley, anxiously. 'But either way, there must be thousands of them by now. Maybe even tens of thousands.'

'You've certainly done your homework,' said Brady, trying to smile.

'It's best to know as much as possible about your enemy.'

'You make it sound like a war.'

Foley grinned cryptically. 'Perhaps it is and the way I figure it, they outnumber us about five hundred to one.'

Brady ran a shaking hand through his hair. 'I'll tell you something else. They're immune to ordinary repellents. I put some down in my garden and it didn't have the slightest effect.'

The curator frowned.

Neither man spoke for long moments then Brady suddenly turned his attention to the worms.

'And those?' he said, pointing to the tray. 'You said they were linked with the slugs. How?'

'Come here,' said Foley, getting up. He led the Health Inspector to a nearby microscope. There was already a slide set up beneath the powerful lens and Brady squinted down the eyepiece, adjusting the focus until everything merged into crystal clarity. Floating around before him were dozens of minute, hairlike organisms which, on closer inspection, he saw resembled tiny versions of the two worms which lay in the tray.

'What are they?' he asked.

'Schistosomes,' said Foley. 'Blood flukes. They're a type of parasite found in the blood stream of slugs. I took that sample from one of our slugs but they're found in every species.'

Brady stepped back from the microscope.

'I still don't see the tie-up,' he said.

'The schistosomes live inside the slugs, right? Now, if a slug is accidentally eaten, even if it's only the tiniest fraction of it, those parasites somehow transmit themselves to the human blood stream. They travel to the brain and form cysts. The worms grow inside these cysts.'

Brady swallowed hard as the curator continued.

'The disease is called Schistosomiasis. Once the worms encyst in the brain it causes nausea, headaches and, more often than not, death.' He paused. 'And there are at least three documented cases in Britain every year.'

'The that was what happened to the bloke in the restaurant.'

Foley nodded. 'He must have, somehow, eaten part of one of the slugs. Everything about these bloody things is bigger or more lethal, it stands to reason the strain of disease carried by them is going to be more virulent.'

Brady sat down heavily. 'And the more of them there are, the more people they're likely to infect.' He sighed. 'The slime trails I kept seeing, Ron Bell's body and now this. It's been slugs all along.'

Foley nodded. 'Should we tell the police?'

'What the hell can they do? Arrest the damn things? Besides, if we went to them and said that there was a plague of killer slugs in the town they'd probably lock us up.'

'I wouldn't blame them,' said Foley, sardonically.

Brady drummed on the desk top with his fingers. 'So what the hell do we do?' He glanced across at the dead worms.

'I can try and perfect a poison of some kind,' Foley offered. 'Something we can use on them but, like I said, there must be thousands by now. And,' he paused, 'if they are using the sewers to move around in, they must be everywhere.'

The words hung ominously in the air and Brady felt cold fingers of fear plucking at the back of his neck.

Eighteen

Clive Talbot fiddled with the controls of the Ferguson hi-fi, trying to find the button which activated the record player. Perplexed by the profusion of dials and buttons which faced him he turned to face Donna Moss, who sat on the sofa.

'How does this fucking thing work?' grunted Clive, still holding the record in one hand.

Donna smiled inanely at him, put down her glass of Bacardi and crossed to the set. She flicked a switch and the turntable buzzed into life.

'Smart arse,' said Clive, dropping the record into position. He watched Donna make her stumbling way back to the sofa then flop down. There was a half empty bottle of Bacardi at her feet which she had drunk since eight o'clock. He noted that the solid silver carriage clock on the mantelpiece said nine fifteen p.m. Clive adjusted the volume as a thunderous bass line roared out of the twin speakers and the singer's voice rose over the strident wail of guitars.

'… what did I see? Could I believe, that what I saw that night was real and not just fantasy'.

Satisfied with the volume, he got to his feet and slouched across to the sofa where he flopped down beside Donna. She looked round and moved towards him, her mouth seeking his, the taste of liquor strong on her tongue as it sought the warm moistness of his own. Clive responded fiercely, simultaneously sliding one hand up the inside of her skirt until he felt it brush the cool material of her panties. Donna pulled away, giggling.

'Stop it,' she said, her face flushed.

'What would your old man say if he could see us now?' said Clive, a triumphant grin on his face.

Donna shrugged and downed what was left in her glass.

'He'd probably be more annoyed to think we were using his hi-fi,' she giggled.

'Yeah, I bet he fucking would.' There was a sharp vehemence in the youth's words and his hard eyes scanned the sitting room as he spoke. He could just imagine the look on old man Moss's face if he could see his daughter now, lying across the lap of a boy he hated. Clive had never got on with either of Donna's parents. Toffee-nosed bastards they were, thought themselves a cut above the rest of the neighbourhood. Just because James Moss was on the town council and Clive's dad worked on a building site, Moss looked down on his daughter's boyfriend with ill-disguised contempt. Many times he'd tried to break up their relationship but each time they'd found a way to continue seeing each other. He'd been going out with her for over a year and she had become something of a habit. Maybe he was in love, he didn't know. Even if he was he'd certainly never let Donna know and if any of his mates should find out he wouldn't dare show his face. At eighteen, Clive Talbot was at that age when overt concern for the opposite sex was something to be frowned on. As far as his little circle of friends were concerned, girls were good for only one thing.

That was certainly true of Donna. She was a year younger than Clive but her sexual precocity bordered on nymphomania and that fact further amused the young man when he thought what her father would say if he found out his 'darling' daughter had lost her virginity at the age of thirteen. To one of Clive's mates as a matter of fact.

Clive himself was an only child and lived with his parents less than half an hour's walk from where Donna lived. It used to be a ten-minute ride on his Yamaha 250 but some bastard had nicked the fucking thing about a month ago. Clive still fumed inwardly as he thought about it but he'd find out who took it and, when he did, he'd make them sorry. He wouldn't go to the police. They were bloody useless and, besides, he'd been in trouble with them a couple of times himself. Only minor offences like breaking windows or fighting but, even so, he had no desire to seek their assistance in retrieving his stolen bike.

It had been an eighteenth birthday present from his parents. All his mates had bikes but most of them had farting little Puch Maxis or puny 150s. Nothing like Clive's. One or two of them even had jobs. Clive himself hadn't worked since he left school two years earlier. He'd looked for work sure enough, he never stopped looking, but his father's often voiced opinions about a Government *for* the rich *by* the rich were rapidly beginning to dawn on him. He'd never listened much to what either of his parents said but his father was shop steward for his branch of the Building Workers Union and, during the past two years, Clive had come to realize that his old man's hatred of the Government was well- founded. Clive now looked across at the photo of James Moss which stood on the TV and felt the anger rising within him

'When are your parents due back?' he asked.

'Late,' Donna said, vaguely.

'Well how late is late?' he said, irritably.

'About two in the morning,' she informed him, reaching once more for the Bacardi bottle. But Clive got to it first and lifted it from her clutching grasp.

'I think you've had enough,' he said, putting the bottle out of reach.

She pouted for a second then reached up and pulled him towards her. 'Perhaps I can persuade you to give it back.'

She pressed her mouth to his, her tongue forcing its way past his teeth and he responded with equal enthusiasm. He felt a tingle run through him as one of her hands fell to the rapidly growing bulge in his jeans. Donna ran her hand over his groin, squeezing his erection through the worn material of his denims. Their mouths still locked together, he reached for the buttons on her blouse and skilfully undid them, his fingers brushing against the lace of her bra. With practised movements, he reached round and undid the clasp, pulling the garment free to expose her small, taut breasts.

She tugged at his belt irritably when it wouldn't come free and Clive finally had to help her, loosening his own button. Donna giggled softly and plunged her hand down inside his underpants, gripping his swollen shaft. Clive squirmed and thrust it forward into her eager, pumping, hand.

He reached across and cupped one small breast in his hand, rubbing his thumb back and forth across the nipple until he felt it stiffen. Donna sighed and, taking hold of his free hand, she thrust it beneath her skirt as if guiding him. But Clive needed no prompting and soon his eager hand was flicking against the flimsy material of her panties. He stroked the silky fabric, feeling the first hint of moisture seeping through it as he pressed harder. Donna gasped and manoeuvred herself so that he could reach her pulsing desire more easily, she felt his probing digits glide through her soft pubic hair to the hardened bud of her clitoris and she felt a comforting warmth envelop her. For her own part, she lowered her head to Clive's lap, her mouth closing over his swollen penis. He sucked in a shaking breath as he felt the hot wetness gliding up and down his shaft. He continued to move his fingers, plunging deeper until he infiltrated her sleek cleft.

Donna flicked her tongue over his bulging penis and she felt the unmistakable twitchings as he neared his climax. He stiffened and grunted and it was at that point she withdrew her head and sat up.

'What the fuck are you doing?' gasped Clive, his face flushed.

Donna smiled impishly. 'Upstairs eh?' she said.

'You are a right cow at times,' he said, panting.

'But lovely with it,' she giggled. 'Do I get my drink now?'

He gave her the bottle, doing up his trousers with difficulty. Clive looked at her once more his anger and frustration quickly disappearing. He chuckled to himself.

'What's so funny?' Donna wanted to know.

'You,' he said. 'If your fucking old man knew what you were like he'd have a stroke.'

'I think mum would like to lock me up in a convent,' Donna said, giggling.

Clive shook his head and watched her as she drank. Her blouse was still off, revealing her breasts and her long, brown hair was unkempt and ruffled. It dangled over her shoulders as she shook her head and she ran one hand through it. The perm was starting to grow out and, only at the top and sides. did it still retain curls

She wore no make-up, except a little on her eyes and, when she looked at him, those twin blue orbs held him in a hypnotic stare.

Maybe he really *was* in love, after all.

Donna sipped her drink and exhaled deeply. She glanced at the clock on the mantel and it said ten p.m. She knew her parents wouldn't be back for a good four or five hours. She and Clive had plenty of time. She watched him as he got to his feet to turn the record over then, a second later, the room was shaken once more by a series of drum and guitar blasts which threatened to reach seismic proportions. She motioned to him to turn the volume down a little which he did.

Donna, unlike Clive, had stayed on at school to study for 'A' levels. She knew that her future was already mapped out for her and there seemed little she could do to alter it. After school it would be university then, hopefully, into a job in designing. She was studying Graphic Design at school and intended gaining a degree once she reached university. But, although Donna wanted the career of her own choosing she still felt a kind of unseen manipulation. The university bit was as much for her parents' sake as her own. She could just hear them at the Rotary club luncheons:

'Oh yes, our daughter is at university.'

Both were fulfilling their own failings through her and she resented it. Of course she would never do anything to hurt their feelings or to damage her own chances of success but, sometimes, she felt the mad urge to say stuff it and walk out of school right there and then. To hell with everything.

Clive was the only thing she really cared about and that was another thing which rankled with her parents. She knew how they felt about him but she would not give him up. No matter how many times her father told her she wasn't to see the young lout (his favourite description of Clive) she always found some way of being with him. In a different kind of way, she was as trapped in her lifestyle as Clive was in his. Both knew how their futures were going to turn out, he because he was unable to get a job and she because she was fulfilling the aspirations of her parents. There seemed no way out.

'...Not a prisoner, I'm a free man, live my life how I want to. Don't care, where the past was, I know where I'm going...'

roared the singer on the record and the words sounded all the more pertinent to Donna. She swallowed what was left in her glass and got to her feet.

'Come on,' she said, smiling, motioning towards the stairs and, in a second, Clive was behind her.

Laughing, they made their way up to Donna's bedroom.

The first half a dozen of the slugs slithered across the glass top of the large cold frame, their posterior tentacles moving silently in the night air. On the ground nearby were many more of them, a shapeless black blot on the dark earth. They slithered over James Moss's carefully tended garden all seemingly heading for one spot.

Moving as quickly as their bloated forms would allow them, the slugs slipped into the drain, crawling up the pipe itself towards the first floor of the house where they eventually emerged in the guttering which ran alongside the windows.

They filled the pipe, overflowed like thick black rain into the guttering and then, slowly, they slid across the brickwork until they were actually on the window sill of the bedroom which faced the back garden. There were many of them and they slid over the sill, dropping to the floor of the bedroom. The darkness in there was total and it was quiet, only the slight murmur of the night breeze breaking the solitude as it set the curtains gently billowing.

The slugs continued to flood into the room.

As Donna and Clive reached the landing they paused, kissing fiercely again, his eager hands searching for her breasts once more but she knocked them away and wagged a reproachful finger at him.

'Wait,' she giggled.

Clive crossed the landing towards a door which was firmly closed.

'Wrong room, idiot,' said Donna, her hand pausing on the knob of her own door.

'I know,' Clive said. 'Is this your parents' bedroom?'

Donna nodded and crossed to the door, pushing it open. She flicked on the light and walked in. Clive followed her, his heavy shoes making deep indentations on the thick white carpet. The whole room seemed to be white. The walls, the ceiling, the wardrobe unit, the dressing table. Even the bedspread was white. It was liking walking into a blizzard. It smelt of lavender and Clive wrinkled his nose.

'Fucking hell,' he said, crossing to the bed where he saw some clothes laying. He laughed and picked up a pair of large knickers.

'Who wears these?' he said, grinning. 'Your mum or your bloody old man?'

Donna laughed, too, and walked across to the wardrobe unit which dominated one side of the large room. It was covered in mirrors and she studied her reflection for long seconds. Clive noticed.

'Mirrors, eh?' he said. 'Kinky bastards aren't they? It's a wonder they haven't got them on the ceiling too.' He made a loud whooping noise and leapt onto the bed, stretching out on it with his arms folded behind his head. 'This is comfortable. Shall we do it here?' he asked, grinning.

Donna giggled. 'Come on, or they'll know someone's been in here.'

She stepped closer and Clive shot out a hand in an attempt to grab her but Donna stepped back and he missed, overbalanced and fell off the bed. Both of them began laughing and Donna hurried to the door and flicked off the light leaving him in darkness.

'You bitch,' he chuckled and chased after her.

He grabbed her just as she reached her own bedroom door and both of them crashed against it laughing like idiots. The door flew open and Donna stepped inside. She flicked at the light switch but nothing happened.

'The bloody bulb must have gone,' she said, snapping the switch up and down.

The room was in complete darkness, only the light which flooded in from the landing lighting their way. Clive closed the door behind him and turned the key, locking it.

'Who needs lights?' he said, and tossed the key away.

Donna giggled and held him close, relaxing as he lowered her onto the bed. In the blackness, they undressed one another until their naked forms lay side by side on the bed.

The curtains billowed in the breeze and neither noticed the gobs of slime on the window sill.

They sought the pleasurable touch of the other's hands, content in the pitch black to give way to almost invisible caresses. Donna felt Clive's hands running over her breasts before sliding down to part her legs which she moved willingly. With her own hand she guided his throbbing erection towards her slippery cleft, gasping when he drove it into her. She locked her legs around his back, increasing the depth of penetration. He began to move rhythmically inside her and she thrust her hips up to meet his every movement, raking his back with her nails. Their grunts and cries became louder as the passion within them grew in intensity.

Neither of them heard the low sucking sounds as the sea of slugs, invisible in the darkness, flowed towards the bed moving almost soundlessly over the carpet.

The eyes of numerous pop stars watched impassively from posters on the walls as the black hordes swept nearer, the warmth and scent of human flesh attracting them.

Donna rotated her hips frenziedly as she felt her orgasm approach and she was mildly disappointed when she felt Clive withdraw from her but that disappointment rapidly disappeared when she felt him sliding further down the bed until his head was resting between her thighs. She moaned with pleasure as his tongue began to flick at her clitoris.

Clive was a tall lad and, in order to position himself correctly, he was forced to allow his feet to drop off the end of the bed. He stretched his legs out behind him, attempting to get a grip on the carpet with his toes.

He almost shouted aloud when he felt his feet touch something wet and slimy.

He raised his head, feeling a jellied movement beneath his toes, then, suddenly, he felt pain lancing through his foot as two of the slugs bit into it.

'Jesus Christ,' he shouted, pulling his feet back onto the bed.

Donna looked down. 'What is it?' she asked, dreamily.

'Something's biting me,' he shrieked.

Donna sat up, her hand reaching for the bedside lamp. She switched it on and, in that same instant she let loose a scream of terror which seemed to fill the entire house. Clive was struggling to remove the monstrous black things from his foot, blood staining the sheets as the foul creatures bored into the flesh.

Donna sat transfixed, watching the black mass of slugs seething towards the bed. A number had already begun to climb up the dangling sheets and Donna screamed again when she saw two near her hand.

With a roar of pain, Clive managed to tear one of the stubborn beasts from his foot. It came away, ripping skin and muscle as it did and he groaned, trying to remove the second. However, the effort made him overbalance and he fell off the bed onto the slippery carpet of slugs. For brief, nauseating seconds he writhed in the slime then the creatures attacked, sinking their sickle shaped teeth into his twisting body. Clive screamed in pain and tried to scramble to his feet.

'Get the fucking door open,' he yelled at Donna who was crying as she watched him struggling with the black horrors, one of which was eating its way into his back.

She sat huddled on the bed, rocking back and forth like a child, her eyes wide and filled with tears.

'The door,' he bellowed, trying to claw the slugs from his back.

But Donna couldn't move and, as more of the vile beasts reached the bed, she felt one crawl onto her hand. It bit into her and she shrieked in pain, feeling the blood running freely from the wound. Another struck at her buttocks, boring deep into the flesh and now Donna struggled to her feet but, a third slug slid up the inside of her thigh and, to her horror, Donna felt it boring into her crutch. She screamed with renewed ferocity as the thick black thing forced its way into her, like some obscene bloated penis. Blood began to flood down the inside of her legs, spraying the carpet and, in a second, the slug had disappeared inside her.

Donna collapsed. Laying across the bed, she was helpless as more of the slugs slid over her body, feeding on the warm flesh and enjoying the distinctive taste of the flowing blood.

Clive saw her body, covered by the beasts and he opened his mouth in a silent scream not sure whether to yell or be sick. His own back felt as if it was on fire as a dozen black creatures ate their way into his muscles. Others were gnawing at his feet and calves but he remained upright, throwing himself against the wall in an effort to dislodge the slugs. A mixture of his own blood and the pulped slugs left a reeking imprint on the nearest poster which regarded the scene of carnage with blank eyes. Clive staggered towards the door, one of the slugs eating into his ear lobe.

He crashed into the bedside lamp and it fell to the floor, plunging the room, once again into impenetrable blackness.

Gritting his teeth, he struggled on, over the slimy sea of blood lusting slugs. The pain in his back and legs was now almost unbearable and he wanted to scream and scream as they tore into him.

He reached the door and crashed against it, one bloodied hand grabbing for the knob.

It was then, through a pain racked brain, he realized he'd locked it. He fumbled for the key, remembering that it lay somewhere in the room.

He shrieked in agonized panic and knew that he must find the key. Must get out.

Must…

The slugs ate through the flesh of his calves and slithered up towards his thighs. He felt the sickness rising inside him and he thought he was going to faint but he punched the door hard, splitting his knuckles. White hot agony lanced up his arm, keeping him conscious. Through eyes filled with tears he saw three or four of the slugs burrowing hungrily into one of Donna's breasts. Her body was still, offering no resistance as the black monstrosities devoured her.

Clive fell to his knees, crushing a number of slugs beneath him as he groped blindly for the lost key. But the black mass covered the floor and his hands only brushed over many thick bodies. One bit into his thumb and he shouted once more in pain. Others were on his thighs now, digging deep into the muscle with their razor sharp teeth. Clive began to weaken, the loss of blood finally slowing him down but still he sought the key, struggling in the darkness.

Some of the other slugs were busily devouring the remnants of their crushed companions, seemingly oblivious to the struggle before them.

Clive groaned despairingly and hauled himself upright, swaying drunkenly for a second. He knew he would never find the key and now, as the black horrors continued to feed on his living flesh, he saw his only hope.

The bedroom window beckoned.

It was a slim hope but his only one and he blundered towards it, arms outstretched. As he reached the window he looked behind him, at the remains of Donna's body. One of the slugs was in the process of eating through her tongue, its obscene form filling her mouth as it feasted.

Clive hoisted himself up onto the sill and, still with a dozen or more of the slugs clinging to him, he jumped.

For seemingly endless seconds he hung in the air as if suspended on invisible wires then, his body plummeted earthward.

He hadn't even had time to think about the cold frame.

Directly beneath Donna's window it glinted as the watery moon shone on the thick glass panels in the top of it and Clive's last sight was of the expanse of glass rushing up to meet him.

He smashed into the cold frame, the panels shattering with an ear-splitting crash. Lumps of jagged glass flew up as if blasted by some kind of explosion, the wood snapped like matchwood and the entire frame collapsed around him.

A shard of glass fully two feet long punctured Clive's body just below the sternum, tearing its way through his chest and erupting from his back. A fountain of blood rose with it. A smaller but no less lethal sliver sliced through his throat and a torrent of crimson gushed from the wound. His body twitched spasmodically, the blood still spurting from the wound in his back, the wind rasping in his torn lung.

Lights flashed on in houses on both sides, faces appeared at windows. Someone dashed for a telephone.

The slugs finished eating and slithered back across the bedroom floor towards the window. Then, as quickly as possible, they made their way back down the drainpipe and down into the drain itself, the familiar blackness and dampness of the sewer beckoning them.

The moon caught the point of the glass shard and it sparkled for a second then faded as Clive Talbot's blood began to congeal on it.

Nineteen

Brady had got home late that evening and Kim was surprised to find that his breath smelt of whisky when he walked in. He had come in at about seven thirty, dropped his briefcase in the hall and then slumped into a chair in the sitting room. The Health Inspector kissed Kim gently on the cheek when she bent over him.

'And where have you been?' she asked, smelling the whisky on his breath. 'There I am slaving over a hot cooker while you're out boozing.' She smiled.

Brady tried to return the gesture but it dissolved away into a sneer. Kim perched on his lap and draped one arm around his neck.

'What's the matter, Mike?' she asked, realizing that there was something wrong. He rarely drank, not unless something was really worrying him.

He shook his head and pulled her closer, loosening his tie with his free hand. 'I just stopped off at the Crown on the way home. I felt as if I needed one.'

She leant closer, sniffing his breath. 'Or two,' she said.

He smiled thinly.

'The dinner's nearly spoiled,' she told him.

'I'm sorry, love,' he said. 'But I'm not very hungry anyway.'

Kim kissed the top of his head, feeling his arm squeezing her more tightly, with an urgency he didn't usually show.

'Are you going to tell me or do I have to drag it out of you?' she said.

'What do you mean?' he asked, looking into her face.

'Come on, Mike. I'm not stupid. What's bothering you?'

Brady exhaled deeply. Should he tell her? The conversation he'd had with Foley that afternoon had unsettled him. No, that wasn't really the word. To hell with it. He was scared. For the first time in his life, and he didn't mind admitting it, Mike Brady was frightened. Not just for himself, but for the rest of the town. And, most of all for Kim. He pulled her closer to him now, wondering whether he should burden her with his newly acquired knowledge. The words whirled around inside his head and he tried to dismiss them as ridiculous. Indeed, the idea of common garden slugs turning on human beings was ludicrous. As was the thought of some of them reaching lengths of six seven and even eight inches. But, he had seen it. He had seen these creatures at first hand and, he had seen what they could do and for fleeting seconds the image of Ron Bell's remains flashed into his mind. The vision of David Watson and those monstrous worms replaced it. But, more than the problem, the solution worried him. How the hell were they going to wipe out the menace? Dare he go to the police with such information?

Brady gently moved Kim from his lap, got to his feet and crossed to the drinks' cabinet. He took out a bottle of Teachers and poured himself a large measure, dropping a couple of ice cubes in as perfunctory afterthoughts. Just to give it the appearance of respectability he thought, taking a hefty swallow. He closed his eyes, feeling the amber liquid burn its way to his stomach. He turned and looked at Kim, holding the bottle before him.

'Join me?' he asked.

She was beginning to get annoyed. 'Mike, please.'

Brady exhaled deeply. 'All right. But what I say now is just between you and me.'

She shook her head, disconsolately. 'Mike, if you can't trust me after all these years…'

'It's not a matter of trust,' he snapped, angrily and she was startled by the vehemence of his outburst. They regarded one another silently for long moments then Brady's tone softened. 'I spoke to Foley this afternoon.' He sighed, sipping at his drink.

'About the slugs?' she said.

He nodded. 'They're ordinary garden slugs:'

'But garden slugs don't attack human beings,' she said.

142

'That's exactly what I said,' echoed Brady going on to repeat his conversation with the curator. Kim listened intently, the hairs on the back of her neck rising slightly.

'Can you be sure about it, Mike?' she asked when he'd finally finished, her voice shaky.

'All the evidence supports my ideas. Foley's investigations just confirmed them,' he said worriedly. He downed the rest of the whisky and poured himself another.

'So you think that Ron Bell was killed by slugs?' asked Kim.

'Yes,' he told her, flatly.

'Then what's to stop them killing someone else?'

His answer sent an icy ripple of fear up her spine.

'Nothing.'

Kim sat back in her chair, the colour drained from her face. She took off her glasses and wiped both eyes and, for a second, Brady thought that she was crying but, as he looked he could see that she wasn't.

'What can you do?' she wanted to know.

He shrugged. 'Foley's working on a new poison. If only, somehow, there were a way of trapping all of the bloody things together in one place perhaps we'd have a chance of destroying them.' He took a hefty swallow from his glass.

'It's hard to believe,' said Kim, softly. She looked at him, her eyes beckoning.

Brady crossed to the chair and sat on the arm, Kim clung to him, her head resting in his lap. He stroked a hand through her hair, conscious that he was shaking slightly.

'There's something else,' he said. 'A man died today at the City Hotel. He died of a disease transmitted by slugs.' The Health Inspector decided to spare her the details.

Kim sat up. 'So the trouble is worse than you first thought?'

He nodded. 'Not only are the slugs themselves attacking human beings, the slime trails they leave contain a lethal fluid and, the man who died ate part of one of them.'

Kim put a hand to her throat. 'Oh God.'

'Foley agrees that they could be using the sewers to move around in. I saw slime trails when I was down there with one of the sewage men.'

'Then they could come up anywhere?'

'Yes.'

She clutched his hand.

'There's nothing we can do at the moment,' he said. 'If I go to the police they'll laugh in my face. We can't put a warning in the papers, people will panic. We'll just have to hope that Foley can perfect a poison in time.'

'In time?' Her words echoed in the room.

'He thinks there must be thousands of them already. We've got to destroy them before they can reproduce in even greater numbers.' He swallowed the rest of his drink.

'Do you think you can?'

Brady walked back towards the drink's cabinet. 'I don't know.' Somewhere, a voice in his head was telling him that they didn't have a hope in hell. The Health Inspector closed his eyes for a moment until the voice went away then he reached for the bottle once more.

Kim got to her feet and walked slowly towards the kitchen.

'You don't want any dinner?' she said, dreamily, the knowledge she had just acquired seeming to have numbed her senses.

Brady smiled and shook his head. He walked back to the chair and flopped into it, the drink held firmly in his hand.

'Kim,' he called and she paused at the kitchen door. 'It'll be all right,' he said but the words sounded empty and reassured neither of them.

She pushed open the kitchen door.

The single scream which she unleashed seemed to shake the house. Brady leapt to his feet, the glass of whisky falling to the floor. He dashed across to her and, together they stood in the doorway, eyes riveted to the sight before them.

Slithering silently over the edge of the stainless steel sink were half a dozen of the slugs. The leading one, a huge monstrosity about six and a half inches in length, had already reached the floor and was sliding across the lino towards the two terrified onlookers. The others were close behind it and, as Brady stepped into the kitchen, he saw more crawling over the edge of the sink, the slime from their bodies making them glisten.

'Get back in there,' he shouted at Kim, pushing her into the sitting room, slamming the door behind him. The Health Inspector snatched up the broom which lay propped against the wall nearby and, using it as a club, he brought it smashing down onto the leading slug. The aim was good and the broom hit its mark. The black creature's body seemed to explode, half of it flying across the kitchen, the eye stalks still waving about silently. Brady stepped past the pulped thing and drove the bristles of the broom against two of the other slugs, watching as they dropped to the floor. He stamped on them, hearing the foul squash as they were scrambled beneath his shoes. Using the broom as a weapon he literally swept the others back over the lip and into the sink itself where, to his horror, he saw dozens more of the creatures slipping and sliding over each other.

One was on the draining board.

The Health Inspector snatched up a carving knife which lay on the drying rack nearby and sliced the foul thing in half. A gout of thick, foul smelling pus-coloured liquid spurted onto his sleeve and he tore his jacket off in disgust. He pushed the severed slug back into the sink with the blade of the knife suddenly realizing how he could destroy them.

He reached for the button which activated the waste disposal unit but his hand wavered as he looked once more into the sink, the horrific realization of how they had got there finally hitting him.

As he watched, one of the slugs eased its obscene black form from the tap.

It hung there for a second then, trailing mucus behind it, the vile beast dropped into the sink. Almost immediately, a pair of eye stalks emerged from the tap, behind it, signalling the arrival of another of the animals.

Disgusted, Brady punched the waste disposal button and the vicious blades roared into action slicing and crushing anything which came their way. Brady used the end of the broom to push the last of the slugs down into the murderous revolving blades, watching with something akin to satisfaction as their bodies were torn and pulped by the machine. He turned on both taps, flushing the last of the black creatures from its hiding place. Propelled by the powerful jet of water, the slug was hurled from the outlet and straight into the grinding jaws of the waste disposal. The water also helped to wash away the evil mixture of pus-like blood and slime which coated the bottom of the sink.

Brady left the taps and the disposal unit running then bolted through the living room and up the stairs, heading for the bathroom.

As he hurtled up the stairs, visions of what he might find whirled through his brain. A bath full of the foul black animals? The whole room seething with them?

He flung open the door.

Nothing.

Breathing a sigh of relief, the Health Inspector crossed to the bath and turned both taps on full blast, the water splashing up violently when it hit the enamel. He watched for long seconds then crossed to the sink, repeating the procedure there.

Once more, there was no sign of the slugs.

Gasping for breath, Brady watched the gushing conduits finally turning them off. He reached for a towel and wrapped it around the sink taps, blocking the outlet. Then he repeated the procedure with those on the bath. Satisfied that they were secure, he hurried back downstairs. Kim looked up at him as he passed, her eyes red and puffy. Brady, breathless from his exertions and also from fear, walked back into the kitchen and switched off first the taps and then the waste disposal unit. A sudden silence descended. Only the Health Inspector's low, guttural breathing interrupting the solitude. As he fastened dishcloths around both taps, he could hear Kim in the sitting room, sobbing softly.

His task completed, he stepped back, nearly treading in the pulped mess behind him. All that remained of the slug he'd killed with the broom. He stepped back until he was leaning against the kitchen wall, his breath now slowly returning to normal.

'Mike.'

He heard Kim's subdued plea and hurried into the sitting room. She was crouching on the floor beside one of the chairs. He knelt beside her, enfolding her in his arms, rocking backward and forward as if he were comforting a child. She held him tightly, her tears staining his shirt.

'Mike,' she repeated.

'It's all right,' he said, reassuringly but couldn't resist a sly glimpse over his shoulder at the kitchen taps.

If the bastards were using the water pipes to move about in too, there was no telling where the horror would end.

Or even *if* it would.

The entire water supply of Merton could be contaminated. The thought hit Brady like a sledgehammer and he swallowed hard.

Kim looked up at him, her eyes red and bloodshot. Her glasses were steamed up and Brady removed them, wiping the big salt tears away with one finger. He held her tightly.

Brady could feel her shaking but he gripped her firmly, wondering if she could feel the powerful shudders which racked *his* body.

Twenty

Charlie Barnes struck the match, his face momentarily illuminated by the yellow light. He tossed it away, hearing it hiss on the damp grass. He sucked hard on the roll-up, leaning against the tree impatiently. The hands on the church clock had crawled on to one fifteen a.m., bathed in the cold white light of the moon, they stood out starkly against the stone face of the clock. The weather vane at the top of the spire rocked gently back and forth in the cool breeze, its squeaking carrying a long distance in the stillness of the night.

Charlie watched the metal clock hands for a few more minutes and then decided that it was now or never. He walked slowly from his hiding place behind the trees, heading towards the open grave which lay about twenty yards from him. He kept to the grassy verges, conscious of the noise his boots would make on the gravel of the path. But, he reasoned to himself, who the hell would be up and about at twenty past one in the morning? And especially in a bloody graveyard. He forgot his caution and chose the path instead, his heavy tread rattling the pieces of shale. It sounded like someone walking over a hundred bags of crisps.

His spade propped over his shoulder like some kind of mock rifle, Charlie marched up to the open grave and peered in. The moonlight glinted on the polished wooden surface of the coffin and, for a second, he could see himself reflected in it. He stood beside the grave, finishing his fag. One large lump of ash fell from the end and dropped onto the coffin lid. What the hell, Charlie thought, it wasn't going to bother the poor sod inside was it? He smiled and dropped the roll-up, grinding it out beneath his boot. Then, he rubbed his hands and drove the spade into the mound of earth at the graveside.

Charlie had been grave digger in Merton's cemetery for the last six years. Ever since he got out of the Scrubs. He'd been in and out of nick all his life, ever since he was a kid and all the people in the town knew him for what he was. But there was nothing malicious about Charlie. No GBH or mugging for him. He hadn't graduated to that, probably never would. His life of crime had consisted of things like nicking bikes or stumbling on things which had fallen from the backs of lorries. At fifty-two, Charlie was treated with something bordering on affection by the older members of Merton. 'A likeable rogue' one of the old ladies used to call him and he smiled at the recollection. The last judge had called him 'an incurable villain'. Charlie grunted indignantly to himself. Silly old sod he thought, remembering how the bastard had sat there, looking at him over the top of his horn-rims like some red robed God with a plaited wig. Charlie had been caught in possession of fifty cases of Johnny Walker which had disappeared from a warehouse in Milchester, about twenty miles away. It hadn't been a case of a quick trip to the magistrate's court and a hundred quid fine (his sentence for having stolen three lawn mowers from the local garden shop). No, this time, he was hauled up to a Crown Court. The case had only taken two days and the end result had been that he'd got eighteen months in the Scrubs. A bit harsh Charlie had thought at the time but, at least, while he was in there he had had time to catch up with a couple of old friends. He smiled to himself.

When he'd come out of jail he'd returned to Merton and, much to his surprise, the local vicar had offered him the job as grave digger. Naturally he had jumped at the chance, although wondering why the old boy was so forthcoming with his offer. Charlie guessed that the vicar saw it as some kind of spiritual exercise - forgive sinners and all that. Charlie smiled to himself. Maybe it had worked because, since becoming town grave digger, he hadn't been in trouble with the law.

But, then again, dead bodies didn't make very good witnesses.

The idea had first come to Charlie after he'd seen a body laid out in the Chapel of Rest, just prior to a funeral some four years ago. The body had been of a man in his seventies and, before any mourners arrived, Charlie had wandered into the Chapel and looked into the open coffin. The body was to be buried with all its jewellery, including a gold and diamond ring which Charlie reckoned must be worth at least £500. He'd stood in awe, gazing at the glittering prize, wondering how much he could get for it if he ever managed to flog it. The point was, how could he get it? Then, that night, lying on his bed smoking, he'd had a brainwave. Along with the job of grave digger came a small wooden building which was little more than a three roomed hut. It stood just inside the main gate of the cemetery and Charlie had made it his home for the last six years. He was also entrusted with locking up the gates at night, a job which had to be done from the inside. So, from ten p.m. onwards, he was effectively sealed inside the cemetery. It became his domain. He was king and, as monarch he intended claiming any treasure which might lie in his mouldering kingdom.

That night, four years ago, he'd dug up the coffin, removed the lid and taken the ring from the finger of the corpse. Unfortunately, it had been a tighter fit than he'd anticipated and Charlie had winced a little when he had to sever the finger with his pocket knife. Still, what the hell, he'd collected a couple of solid gold cuff links and a diamond tie-pin too from his generous benefactor. On his next day off, Charlie had taken his little hoard up to an old friend in London. One 'Spider' Wyatt, a fence. Spider had given Charlie 900 quid for the little package, a sum which the fence knew he could recoup three times over. Unbeknownst to Charlie, the ring had been antique. But, it had been the beginning of a blossoming little business venture. Ever since that first night, Charlie had been pillaging the dead of Merton for anything he thought valuable. Just a perk of the job he thought happily as he jumped down into the open grave, screwdriver in hand.

He usually had to wait until this time to do his little job and, if the body had already been buried, it sometimes took him until four a.m. to complete his task of exhuming and then re-burial. Sometimes of course he was unlucky but, on most occasions he found something worth taking and, just lately, he'd taken to inspecting the mouths of the corpses for gold teeth. The yield had been unexpectedly fruitful, although he had to confess, prizing the teeth from dead mouths was something he hadn't quite come to terms with yet. But, he put up with the smells and the clammy touch of the bodies. He collected his prizes, hiding them carefully in a locked box beneath his bed. Then, once a month, he'd take a trip up to London and see what he could get for his latest haul. Spider had asked him once where he acquired the stuff and, giggling like an idiot, Charlie had told him. The fence had paled on hearing the news but, goods were goods in his game and the source of these particular valuables made them untraceable.

Charlie grinned to himself as he inserted the screwdriver in the slit of the first screw. Things had definitely begun to look up during the last four years. Or look down as the case may be. He chuckled to himself and removed the first screw, dropping it into the pocket of his trousers. He'd removed his jacket, despite the slight chill in the air but he knew that filling the hole in would be hard work once he got around to it.

He removed the second of the six screws and wondered what prize he would find tonight. He'd seen a particularly valuable wristwatch on the corpse when it was lying in the Chapel of Rest and there was no telling what else he would find.

Smiling happily, Charlie set to work on the third screw.

Something moved behind him and the sound startled him. His hand slipped and the screwdriver scored a deep furrow across the lid of the coffin.

'Shit,' grunted Charlie and straightened up, peering over the rim of the hole to see what was happening. He strained his ears for the slightest sound, the moon shining coldly down over the cemetery like an enormous flare.

He could see nothing and the only sound he heard was the low wailing of the wind as it sighed in the trees. It sounded like someone whistling tunelessly. Charlie remained upright for a second longer then bent once more and set about the third screw. That finally came free and he pulled it out of the hole and dropped it into his pocket.

The fourth one was a real bastard and seemed to have been wedged in with a power designed to thwart Charlie in his task. He put all his weight behind the screwdriver, trying to move the recalcitrant screw. Muttering to himself, Charlie strained with all his might to remove it, splitting the wood in one place where he bore down too hard. But, eventually, it began to give. He smiled, a thin film of perspiration forming across his forehead. He wiped it away with the back of his hand and set to work on the fifth screw.

That one came away much more easily and he moved towards the last one. The final obstacle between him and his goal.

Again something moved, closer to him this time, and he swallowed hard, his hand shaking for some reason. He wasn't sure whether to straighten up or not.

He remained still, the screwdriver firmly planted in the groove of the screw head.

The sound came again. It was much closer this time - less than ten feet away he guessed.

A thought swept through his mind. Had he remembered to lock the cemetery gates? Had the vicar walked in on him? Charlie strained his ears, trying to catch even the slightest sound. He slowed his breathing, the air stuck in his throat.

Very slowly he rose to his feet, the sound drawing closer. It sounded like a low snuffling, followed, a second later by a high-pitched scratching. Holding the screwdriver like a weapon, Charlie stood up.

He scanned the area around him.

Nothing moved.

Then he saw it, crouched on the marble Plinth in the centre of one grave.

A mouse.

Charlie breathed an audible sigh of relief, angry with himself for being so jumpy. He watched the little mouse as it nibbled at some freshly laid flowers. Charlie was about to return to the coffin at his feet when he heard a screech which froze his blood.

Like a winged torpedo, an owl hurtled out of the night sky and, in one practised movement, snatched up the mouse in a powerful talon. Clutching its prize, it flew off towards one of the nearby trees to eat. Charlie watched it, the moon reflecting in its baleful eyes. It seemed to be watching him, looking up every so often, fixing him in that glassy stare. He turned his back on it and ducked down into the grave, removing the last screw. That done, he dug his fingers under the lid and lifted it free, pushing it up onto the side of the hole.

He looked down.

Had he been able to, Charlie would have probably screamed, as it was, he could only stand transfixed gazing down into the coffin, his mind reeling. He gagged and fell back against the grave wall.

The corpse was completely hidden beneath a slimy, seething black mass of slugs.

The stench which emanated from this vast horde was almost palpable in its intensity and Charlie tried to turn away but, with the same sort of deadly fascination with which a mongoose watches a cobra, he kept his gaze locked on the hideous sight before him. His hesitation proved to be his undoing.

A number of the slugs had already slithered over the edge of the coffin and two or three were sliding up Charlie's boots, up inside his trouser legs, heading for the warm flesh of his calves. He felt the sticky slime on his legs and, a second later, he screamed as the slugs bit into him. Blood began to course down his legs as the beasts burrowed deep into his muscles and Charlie groped at the side of the grave, trying to pull himself up but, as he turned, he stepped on one of the monstrous slugs. Its body was crushed under his boot and Charlie slipped in the pulped mess.

With horror, he realized he was falling.

He pitched forward, falling right into the middle of the slithering mass, into the coffin itself. He lay on top of the devoured corpse and, for nauseating seconds found himself staring into the skeletal face which seemed to grin up at him from its silk-lined box.

Charlie screamed again and tried to rise, dozens of the slugs clinging to his body, boring into his flesh. Eating him alive. He pulled a couple from him, horrified when they turned in his grip and drove their razor sharp central teeth into his fingers. He shook his hands in an effort to dislodge the creatures but they remained firmly anchored. Charlie felt something ripping at the muscles of his back, eating through to his kidneys. His back was covered in the vile things, the weight of their thick bodies holding him down. With a monumental effort, he rose, tears of pain and terror mingling with the blood on his cheeks as one of the slugs ate its way into his face. He grabbed a tuft of grass at the grave side and tried to haul himself up but his arms were weak. Blood gushed from his many wounds and he could feel nothing from the knees downward.

The slugs had already eaten his legs to the bone.

He managed to haul himself up, his upper torso actually leaving the hole but then the sheer weight of the creatures defeated him and, as a particularly large one began to burrow into the hollow at the base of his skull, he slipped back. He crashed heavily into the grave, falling once more onto the devoured corpse, his body twitching now as the slugs swarmed over him, one of them eating through the fluid filled cavity of his eye. Blood burst from the socket and Charlie found himself in darkness.

The last thing he saw was the gold wristwatch, dangling on the end of a half-eaten arm, just before his face. Then, with a final wail of despair he succumbed. The slugs slithered over him, seemingly galvanised by the flow of warm blood which pumped from his body.

The owl looked up from its meal as it heard Charlie scream. It sat on the branch of the tree, watching as the man died. Its huge eyes blinked, then it hooted twice, the sound flowing out on the wind like some kind of death knell.

Twenty-one

Mike Brady sat gazing at the phone, a pencil stuck in his mouth like a cigarette. He finally pulled the pencil out and began drawing circles on his blotter. The air conditioner in the office had packed up and the heat was oppressive even so early in the morning. His wall clock showed ten fifteen a.m. He exhaled deeply and reached for the phone, using the end of the pencil to dial. As he did so he thought back to what had happened the previous night. The idea of slugs in the water pipes both revolted and horrified him and, once again, he wondered just how far the contamination had spread. Before he and Kim had left for work that morning he'd secured all the taps with rags. Just in case. Kim, still slightly shaken by the previous night's occurrence, had promised that she would insist all water used at the nursery would be boiled before use. He had given her some story about mould in the pipes in case any of the other staff asked why.

The line was engaged and Brady tapped the pencil irritably on his desk. He let the insistent tone continue for another moment or two then pressed the cradle down and dialled again.

It was still engaged.

'Come on,' he muttered, trying his luck a third time.

At last he heard the familiar purring and he put down his pencil, waiting for the receiver to be picked up. A moment later an officious sounding woman told him that he'd reached the local doctor's surgery.

'My name's Brady,' he told her. 'I'm the Health Inspector. I'd like to speak to Dr Warwick please.'

He was told that the doctor was in surgery.

'It's important, please put me through if you can,' Brady insisted, picking up his pencil once more. He began turning it over and over in his hand.

The receptionist told him again that the doctor was in the middle of his surgery, adding that he had a patient with him at that minute.

'Well can you put me through when that patient leaves, I'll hang on.'

Brady was told that it would have to wait until surgery was finished.

'Listen, you put me through when that next bloody patient has left or I'll be down there myself,' he rasped, finally losing his temper. 'This is important.'

The receptionist reluctantly agreed, swayed by his angry tone and Brady heard her put the receiver down on her desk top. He held his own phone, the far off noises of the surgery drifting through to him. Finally he heard a high pitched bleep and the receptionist picked up the phone and grudgingly told him that he was being connected. There was a moment's silence, a hiss of static then Brady heard another voice.

'Dr Warwick speaking.'

Brady introduced himself. He'd known the doctor for five or six years but the men were still to reach the familiarity of first name terms.

'What can I do for you, Mr Brady? I am rather busy this morning,' Warwick told him.

'I'd like to know if there's been anything unusual this morning,' said Brady.

Warwick was puzzled. 'Like what?'

'Any patients complaining of sickness, headaches anything like that?'

The doctor was mildly irritated. 'Mr Brady, I don't discuss my patients' problems over the phone. In fact, I don't discuss them at all.'

'I realize that,' said the Health Inspector. 'All I want to know is, have there been any peculiarities? Any people suffering from the same symptoms?'

'I cannot divulge personal information, Mr Brady. I'm sorry,' said Warwick, condescendingly.

'I'm not asking for names and addresses for Christ's sake,' snapped the Health Inspector. 'I just want to know if you've had any patients exhibiting the same sort of symptoms, similar symptoms to each other.'

Warwick sighed. 'Mr Brady I...'

'Doctor, this is important. I have reason to believe that the entire water system of Merton could be contaminated. Now, all I'm asking for is a little help. If you don't want to help me, fine, but I'm warning you your bloody surgery is going to be knee-deep in people if you don't.'

There was a long silence at the other end of the line and, for a moment, Brady thought that the doctor had put the phone down but then he spoke again, his tone much more subdued this time.

'What makes you think the water supply is contaminated?' he asked.

'That's information *I* can't divulge,' said Brady.

Warwick chuckled mirthlessly. 'Touché.'

'So, doctor. About your patients, have there been any similarities in their symptoms?'

The doctor exhaled deeply. 'Well, now you come to mention it, there have. I've seen twelve patients since eight thirty and nine of those have been complaining of more or less the same problems.'

Brady reached for his pencil once more, pulling a pad towards him. 'Such as?'

'Nausea, headaches, sensitivity to light, diarrhoea. Fever in one or two cases and some vomiting. Is that enough for you?'

Brady finished writing.

'What do *you* think it is?' he asked.

'It's difficult to say without the benefit of more extended diagnoses such as blood and urine tests but at first sight I'd say it was probably a virus of some kind,' Warwick told him.

'Did you prescribe anything for it?' asked Brady.

'Only a Kaolin solution to stop the diarrhoea and vomiting. As I said, without further tests it's difficult to say what's really causing the trouble.'

'If it was a virus,' said the Health Inspector, 'wouldn't you prescribe antibiotics?'

'That depends on the severity of the symptoms. But, as I've already said, I'm not absolutely sure it is a virus. However, I will admit that if it is, your theory about it being carried by water is probably correct.'

Brady felt icy fingers tugging once more at the back of his neck. 'Why do you say that?'

'Because all water transmitted viral diseases exhibit symptoms like those I've just described to you. But to be honest, Mr Brady, the likelihood of it being a virus is small. Most diseases of that kind are transmitted by animals. Yellow fever by mosquitoes, Bilharzia by snails. Those types of disease are confined to areas where sanitation is bad, you wouldn't find anything like that...'

Brady cut him short. 'You said something about snails.'

'Yes. There is a species of snail which spreads a disease called Bilharzia,' Warwick explained, his voice breaking up into a soft chuckle. 'But it's not that, Mr Brady. The snail which carried the disease is confined to Africa and Asia.'

The Health Inspector wrote it on his pad all the same.

'If there's nothing else, Mr Brady' said the doctor 'I do have other patients waiting.'

'Yes. I'm sorry,' said the Health Inspector. 'Thank you very much for your help.' He put the phone down and sat silently at his desk, reading the notes he'd scrawled:

1. Virus?
2. Water carried, contamination?
3. Nine cases so far.
4. Slugs in water pipes?

He underlined the last several times then got to his feet and headed out of his office towards the stairs which would take him up to the second floor and the offices of the Water Board.

Frank Phillips was trying to light a fag. He had dropped his lighter the day before and now the bloody thing wasn't working. Grunting to himself he put it back into his jacket and started hunting through his pockets for some matches. He found none and plucked the cigarette from his mouth angrily. It lay on the desk before him, defiantly. Phillips was in his late fifties and had been Merton's Water Board Inspector for the last nineteen years. He was a hard; uncompromising man, disliked by nearly everyone in the building but he was good at his job and when he snapped his fingers everyone in the department jumped. He ran a hand through his grey hair and picked up the first of a pile of complaints, glancing over it. He looked at the cigarette lying beside him then continued reading the sheet of yellow paper before him, simultaneously cursing the heat. His shirt was sticking to his back, dark rings of perspiration fanning out from beneath his arm pits. He got up and crossed to the water dispenser which stood in one corner of his office. Phillips took a plastic beaker from the pile beside it and filled it, drinking the clear liquid down in two enormous gulps. He filled the cup again and returned to his desk, reaching for the second sheet of paper in the tray to his left.

There was a knock on the door and Brady walked in.

'You're supposed to wait until you're bloody asked,' snapped Phillips. 'Not just walk in.'

Brady closed the door behind him. 'Yeah, never mind that, Frank, I've got to talk to you.'

'I'm busy, Mike,' he said, indicating the pile of papers.

'It's important,' Brady insisted and Phillips sat back in his chair.

'All right, but make it snappy will you?' he said, then he suddenly remembered the cigarette. 'You haven't got a light have you?' he said, hopefully.

'I don't smoke,' Brady told him.

'I should have guessed,' grunted Phillips.

'Look, Frank, just shut up and listen will you,' Brady said, his voice taking on a hard edge. Satisfied that he had the other man's attention he continued. 'I don't quite know how to say this so I won't beat about the bush.' He inhaled. 'How long would it take to cut off Merton's water supply?'

Phillips raised one eyebrow. 'How long would it what?' he said, incredulously.

Brady repeated himself.

'You are joking of course?' said Phillips, sipping at the cup of water on his desk. 'What the bloody hell should I want to cut off the water supply for?'

'Because there's something in the water,' Brady told him.

'Like what?'

'A virus of some kind.'

159

'How do you know?'

'I phoned the local doctor's surgery this morning,' Brady told him and went on to describe his conversation with Warwick.

'So,' said Phillips. 'Nine people have got the shits, what does that prove?'

'Even the doctor thinks that there could be something in the water,' said Brady.

Phillips sat forward in his chair. 'Yes, there is.' His voice took on a mocking tone. 'There's chlorine which is added as a gas, dissolves and forms a disinfectant. There's sulphur dioxide which is also added as a gas to neutralize any excess chlorine. There's fluoride to keep everybody's teeth in such terrific shape and occasionally, in rotten water, we use aluminium sulphate. Satisfied?'

Brady was white with rage. 'All right you smart arse bastard,' he rasped. 'Nine people are suffering from a virus which they've picked up through drinking water. That's nine people, Frank. From one surgery. There's three others in the town. Christ knows how many more poor sods have got this bloody infection.'

'So, let's get this straight, you want me to turn off the town's water?'

The Health Inspector nodded.

Phillips shrugged. 'Just how did you come to this expert diagnosis in the first place?' asked the Water Board Official, his voice heavy with sarcasm. 'I mean, what made you ring the bloody doctor anyway?'

'Something strange happened at my house last night,' Brady began, aware that the words he was about to speak would sound ludicrous. 'I saw slugs dropping from my taps.'

'Slugs,' said Phillips, nodding.

'Yes.'

Phillips exhaled deeply. 'You want me to believe that there's slugs crawling around in our water pipes is that it? And these unfortunate buggers with the runs have got that way because of these things being in *their* water pipes. Right?'

'I know it sounds incredible,' said Brady.

Phillips laughed humourlessly. 'Incredible? It sounds bloody ridiculous.'

'I saw it,' snapped Brady. 'So did my wife.'

'I couldn't give a damn if the Band of the Coldstream Guards saw it,' snarled Phillips. 'Just assuming I shut off the water. Just assuming. What the hell am I supposed to say to the council when they ask me why I did it? I can just hear it now, "Mr Brady, our wonderful Health Inspector, says we've got slugs in our pipes". You know what this bloody lot think of you already. How the hell is that going to sound?'

'Do you need Council permission to switch it off?' Brady wanted to know.

'I don't *need* it,' Phillips told him. 'But I think they're going to want a better excuse than that. And what do I tell the public when they start ringing in and complaining because they can't make a cup of tea because they've got no bloody water?'

'So you won't do it?'

'No I won't. Not until I see some proof.' He picked up the plastic cup and pushed it towards Brady. 'I can't see anything floating about in there can you?'

'What about those nine people, aren't they proof enough?' snapped the Health Inspector.

'Coincidence,' said Phillips, dismissing it.

'Bullshit,' snarled Brady. 'That's not all, haven't you noticed the amount of slugs in the gardens lately? And another thing, I've seen their trails in three or four different places but on top of that, I told you, I saw them dropping from my taps. Slugs. Big bastards too.' He had lost his temper. 'A man died yesterday from a disease transmitted by slugs.' Brady's voice had risen in volume. 'How much more fucking proof do you want?'

The two men stared at each other in silence for long moments then Phillips smiled. 'Look, I tell you what, if *I* get a case of the runs then I'll know you were right. How's that?'

Brady got to his feet, almost knocking the chair over in his anger. He turned and made for the door, pausing before he reached it.

'You know, Frank,' he said. 'You shouldn't be working for the Council. You should be on it. You're stupid enough.'

He slammed the door behind him.

'Sod off,' grunted Phillips. He sat for a moment then crossed to the water dispenser again and poured himself another cup full of the clear liquid. He looked into it for a second.

'Slugs in the water pipes,' he said, shaking his head.

He drank the water.

Brady glanced at his watch and saw that the hands had crawled round to one fifty-five p.m. He finished his half of lager and got to his feet, leaving the half-eaten remains of a ploughman's lunch on the table before him. The lounge bar of The Ruskin Arms, the only pub in Merton's town centre, was almost empty but for those last half dozen who lingered over their drinks. Brady left the pub, walking from its subdued and dimly lit interior into the blazing sunshine of the afternoon.

It was less than ten minutes' walk from the pub to the council offices and the Health Inspector took it slowly. A barmaid was outside the pub collecting empty glasses and she smiled at Brady as he passed but it was an effort for him to return the gesture. He wiped the perspiration from his face and glanced up at the cloudless sky. The heat was unrelenting and Brady stopped at a small newsagent's nearby to purchase an ice-cream. He felt mildly ridiculous standing amidst dozens of kids, waiting for his chance to be served and he had to smile at the thought of what he must look like. The woman serving smiled broadly at him when he asked for a lolly. He handed over his money and eagerly tore off the wrapping. The ice-cream was pleasantly cool on his tongue.

It was as he was walking out, Brady noticed the newspaper rack which hung by the door. He scanned the dailies but his eye settled on the local paper. With one hand, Brady pulled it from the rack and ran his eyes over the headline:

POLICE BAFFLED BY MYSTERY DEATHS

He swallowed hard, folded the paper under his arm and tossed ten pence onto the counter. Then he walked out. On the way out, he dropped the ice-cream into a dustbin, as if he had suddenly decided he didn't want it. Brady paused outside the shop and scanned the article which accompanied the headline.

'Merton Police were baffled today after finding three mutilated bodies. The first two were discovered in a house on the town's new estate, the third in the cemetery. All three were badly mutilated and identification is still unsubstantiated regarding the third body. The other two have not yet been named. Policemen in the area are still looking for clues to the grisly trio of deaths...'

Brady folded the paper again and stood for a moment beneath the blazing sun, the thoughts whirling round and round in his mind. The cemetery. The new estate. They were nearly four miles apart. The slugs must be far more numerous than even *he'd* first thought. He shivered, despite the heat, then turned and headed back towards the council offices.

Brady walked with ill-disguised haste, almost as if he were anxious to be off the streets and back in the security of his office. He felt almost unaccountably nervous, wondering just where the slugs were going to strike next.

There was something black about two feet away from him and Brady froze. It was lying motionless on the pavement, and for long seconds the Health Inspector was unable to move. Then, he realized that it was nothing more than a burnt out dog-end. He breathed an audible sigh of relief and continued walking, reaching the steps that led up to the main doors of the council offices at exactly five past two. As he walked into reception he heard the familiar clacking of the defective fan but it still offered some welcome respite from the blistering sun outside.

Brady was heading for the stairs when Julie appeared from behind the desk and called him over.

'What is it?' he asked, wearily.

'There was a phone call for you, Mr Brady,' she told him. 'A man. He said it was important. He left a phone number.'

'Did he leave his name?'

She consulted a piece of paper in front of her, finally discovering it amongst numerous other jottings and scribbles.

'Foley. John Foley '

Brady was already gone before she could finish speaking.

Twenty-two

Brady looked down into the tray where Foley had placed the slug. The animal was slithering about in a puddle of its own slime and the Health Inspector regarded it with a mixture of disgust and foreboding. Beside the tray was a small beaker filled with a thin, orange coloured fluid and it was into this that Foley now pushed a dropper. He sucked up about half an inch of the stuff into the dropper and Brady watched as he moved it over until it was poised above the slug.

'Watch,' said Foley then, gently, he squeezed the rubber bulb at the end of the dropper.

One single droplet of moisture fell from the nozzle and onto the slug.

There was a tiny flash of brilliant white light and Brady heard a loud hiss as the fluid hit the slug. The black body seemed to explode and a small shower of pus-like blood and entrails sprayed into the air. It writhed spasmodically for a second then was still.

'Good God,' gasped the Health Inspector.

Foley looked up at him and smiled.

'Is it dead?' asked Brady, peering closer to the body.

'Too right it's dead,' Foley reassured him.

'What is that stuff?' He pointed to the beaker full of fluid.

'It hasn't got a name. I invented it,' the naturalist beamed. 'Perhaps I ought to call it Foleycide.' He laughed.

'Well, whatever you call it, it certainly works. But what made it explode like that?'

'The liquid itself is arsenic based but it's got a strong lithium content. Lithium is combustible if it touches any kind of moisture. If you emptied ten or twelve gallons of it into a lake you'd have an explosion big enough to flatten this town.' He grinned triumphantly.

'Where the hell did you get the chemicals?' Brady wanted to know, his eyes still riveted to the ruptured body of the slug.

'The factory on the industrial estate,' Foley told him. 'I told them it was for use in the museum, they let me have as much as I wanted for trade price.'

'How much have you got?'

'Enough,' said the curator.

'I hope to Christ you're right,' Brady said and handed the paper to Foley. He read the article about the three deaths, his brow wrinkling as he did so.

'They got into my house last night,' said the Health Inspector. 'Dozens of them.'

'The slugs? How?'

'Through the taps. They're using the water pipes as well as the sewers to move around in.'

Foley dropped the paper. 'Then how the hell do we kill them all? We can pump this stuff into the sewers without any problem, that'll take care of the ones in there but not into the water system.'

'If what you say about this stuff being combustible when it makes contact with water is true, I'm not even sure that we can use it in the sewers.'

The curator stroked his chin thoughtfully for a second.

'The flash that you saw when the poison hit the slug,' he began. 'It looked worse than it actually was. Maybe, just maybe, we can use it in the sewers and not do too much harm.'

'By too much harm I suppose you mean demolishing the whole of Merton,' said Brady, cryptically.

'There's got to be a way,' said Foley. 'But who the hell would know?'

Brady snapped his fingers. 'Palmer.'

Foley looked vague. 'Who?'

'Don Palmer. He's one of the sewage men here. I was with him when I saw the slime trails down the sewers on the new estate. He'd know whether we could use the stuff down there or not.'

The Health Inspector smiled as he thought about the little cockney. 'Have you got a phone in here?'

'At the enquiries desk,' the naturalist told him.

Brady turned and headed for the door, pausing when he got there. 'You said it contained arsenic too.'

Foley nodded. 'It works two ways. Initial contact causes the reaction you and I just saw, the arsenic penetrates their skin. It works instantly. There's no way they can survive this.' He brandished the beaker full of orange liquid before him.

Brady left the room and made for the enquiries desk where he found the phone and hurriedly dialled.

The phone was picked up at the other end and he recognised Julie's voice.

'Is Don Palmer there?' he asked.

She told him she'd check.

Brady drummed on the desk top as he waited. A second later, Julie picked up the receiver again.

No. Palmer was out on a job.

'Well, as soon as he gets back, tell him to come to the museum,' said the Health Inspector. He put the phone down and hurried back up to the lab.

'No luck,' he said, plonking himself down on a stool. 'We'll have to wait for him.' He looked down at the torn body of the large slug in the tray and shuddered.

'I've been thinking,' said Foley, 'what if these slugs have some kind of social order?'

Brady looked vague. 'What do you mean?'

'Well, maybe, and it's a long shot, the larger slugs are acting as...' he struggled for the word, '...guides, leaders for the smaller ones. Maybe it's some kind of,' he paused again, 'sonar.'

'Where's your evidence?' asked Brady.

'It's supposition at the moment but it's all we've got. Now, assuming that I'm right about the larger slugs being "controllers" of the smaller ones. If we can destroy the large creatures, the others might return to their normal behaviour patterns.'

'You mean they'd stop eating meat?' said Brady.

Foley nodded.

'But how do we destroy them?'

'The large ones are too big to move through the water pipes, right? That means they must be using the sewers to breed and move about in.'

'What's this business about a "social order". got to do with it?' asked Brady.

'Ants and other social insects have a hierarchy within the nest,' Foley explained. 'From the queen down to the soldiers and then to the workers. The queen and the soldiers "control" the smaller workers. Kill the queen, the nest dies.'

The Health inspector shook his head. 'But slugs aren't social insects. Christ Almighty, they're not even bloody insects.'

Foley waved a hand before him. 'I know that. But the principle is the same. There's no nest and there's no queen but I'm pretty sure that the large slugs are acting as "controllers" for the small ones and I'm willing to bet that they're using the sewers as breeding grounds. The conditions down there are perfect.'

'I can't believe this,' said the Health Inspector. 'I've seen it, I've read about what they can do but I still find it hard to believe.'

'And so will everyone else,' intoned Foley. 'Have you mentioned it to anyone?'

Brady told him about the incident with Phillips and then went on to discuss the cases of illness which the doctor had told him about.

'We can't involve the police,' he said, finally.

'They are involved,' snapped Foley, holding up the paper.

'They don't know about the slugs,' said Brady. 'And they mustn't know about the poison or our attempts to destroy these things.'

Foley nodded then laughed bitterly. 'You know, for the first time in my life I thought about dying. Stupid isn't it?' He looked up and found Brady regarding him with impassive eyes. The curator continued.

'After reading what happened to those three people...' The sentence trailed off momentarily. 'Whatever must it be like to die like that?' He swallowed hard.

'Let's just hope none of us have to find out,' said Brady.

The curator reached into a cupboard beside him and produced a bottle of vodka. He held it up, smiling.

'Well, the water's off isn't it?'

Brady grinned, watching as the young man poured some of the clear liquor into two beakers. He handed one to the Health Inspector who drank deeply. The fiery liquid burnt a path to his stomach and he blew out his cheeks.

'How much of that poison have you got?' he asked.

'Enough to make up five gallons,' Foley told him. 'Our only other problem is how to get it into the sewer. We can't just pour it into the first outlet we find.'

'Palmer should be able to help us there.' Brady looked at his watch. 'Where the hell is he?'

'Someone is going to have to go into the sewer tunnels,' said Foley, softly.

Brady didn't answer, he just took another swallow of vodka. That particular thought had already occurred to him.

It was nearly seven thirty p.m. when Don Palmer finally arrived. He parked the white van outside the museum between Foley's Volkswagen and Brady's Vauxhall then walked up the steps to the main entrance.

In his years of living in the town, Palmer had never visited the museum and now he walked slowly through the lower gallery, admiring the handsomely mounted exhibits and making a mental note to bring the kids along some time. They'd enjoy this, he thought. The little cockney made his way up the stairs to the enquiries desk, his footsteps echoing through the silent building.

As he reached the landing Brady appeared in the doorway of the lab and beckoned Palmer up.

'What's wrong?' he asked, grinning. 'Have they got a badger stuck down the toilet?'

Brady ushered him into the lab where he was hastily introduced to Foley. The men all sat down again and Palmer gratefully accepted the beaker of vodka which the young curator offered him.

'My old lady will think I've been out boozing,' he said, smiling, taking another sip of the liquor. It was as he put the beaker down that he noticed the dead slug.

'What the fuck is that?' he said in awe, his mouth dropping open. He looked first at Foley and then at the Health Inspector.

'It's a slug,' Foley told him.

'Leave it out,' Palmer said, his smile gradually dissolving. 'Slugs are little things about that size.' He held open his thumb and index finger to indicate the length he spoke of.

'Have you seen the paper?' Brady asked him, pushing it towards him.

Palmer nodded. 'Terrible business.'

'They were killed by slugs,' said the Health Inspector flatly. 'All three of them and Ron Bell, he was killed by them too.'

'I knew old Ron,' said the cockney, softly. Then his voice took on a harder edge. 'Killed by slugs? Is that some sort of bloody joke?'

They told him. Step by step, every incident, every sighting, every death. Brady told him about the slime trails, about the creatures in his garden, of how one tried to bite him. About the taps.

Foley explained how they fed, moved and bred. Palmer listened to every word, his face set in an attitude of horrified resignation as if that was the way it was and he would just have to get used to it. He paled visibly as the catalogue of horrors continued.

They told him about the poison and about how they intended destroying the slugs. Foley even gave him a demonstration on the last remaining creature. And the little man listened to it all, waiting until there was no more to be said. Silence descended once more on the small lab and, outside, the sky began to darken for it had taken them well over seventy minutes to tell him everything. Every mind-bending, horrifying, nauseating detail.

'Dear God,' he said, softly. He drank what was left in his beaker and gripped it until the glass threatened to break.

'Dear God.'

'We need your help, Palmer,' said Brady, putting one hand on the sewage man's shoulder.

Palmer shrugged and turned almost robotically to look at the Health Inspector.

'It could have been my kids, my wife,' he said, quietly. Visibly shaken, the sewage man put down the beaker and shook his head.

'How can I help?' he asked.

'We need a map of the sewer system,' Brady told him. 'And we need some information.'

At last, the little cockney seemed to come out of his bewildered state. He shook his head, as if trying to dispel the horror of what he'd heard. 'I've got maps in the van,' he said, getting to his feet.

Foley, too, stood up.

'I'd better make up the rest of that poison,' he said and disappeared into a small room just off from the laboratory itself.

Brady was left alone in the lab. He looked at the body of the dead slug and felt an involuntary shudder run through him. He suddenly felt as if he needed Kim. He would have to phone her soon and try to explain what was happening. She would wonder where he was. He exhaled deeply and leant on the work top.

Moments later, Palmer returned carrying a couple of rolled up pieces of paper. He took off the elastic bands and spread them out on the work top. Brady anchored them at the corners with bottles, beakers and anything else he could lay his hands on and then the two of them began to scrutinise the maps. The plans reminded Brady of the London Underground; lines criss-crossed and intercepted each other, some drawn in red, some in black. There were large red circles on many places on the maps and each was marked with a number.

'What are those?' asked the Health Inspector, pointing to one of the numbered circles.

'Manholes,' said Palmer. 'Each number designates the street it's in.'

'How the hell do you remember which is which?' Brady wanted to know but Palmer merely smiled.

'It's all part of the job.'

A moment or two later, Foley walked back into the lab. He removed a pair of rubber gloves and dumped them on the bench nearby.

'Poison's ready,' he said.

'You reckon you're going to dump that stuff into the sewers?' said Palmer.

'It's the only way,' said Foley.

'There's already a high concentration of methane down there now. That's highly combustible too,' said the sewage man. 'If you set off an explosion down there, it'll ignite the methane as well.'

'What are you saying?' asked Brady.

Palmer exhaled. 'I'm saying that the combined effect of that poison and the methane could cause a class one explosion.'

Brady swallowed hard. 'Oh Christ.'

'Is that for certain?' Foley wanted to know.

'There'll be an explosion,' Palmer told him. 'No doubt about it, all we don't know is what the effects could be. '

'What's the worst that could happen?' asked the Health Inspector.

Palmer shrugged. 'You could blow every manhole cover in town off. If the explosion was big enough you'd blast every water appliance from its housing. You might even bring the street down.'

'Maybe?' said Foley, hopefully.

Palmer nodded. 'That's the worst that could happen. But, every house has a vent outside it. Those vents would take up a lot of the blast. They might just be able to cope with the increased pressure. It all depends on how big the explosion is.'

'Then we'll have to take that chance,' said Brady, flatly.

'So now we have to find them,' Foley said and, for long minutes, the room was plunged into silence.

'The first body was found near the new estate,' said Brady, finally. 'And most of the incidents have happened in that vicinity.' He scanned the map. 'Where would that be on here?'

'Ron Bell's house you mean?' Palmer said and jabbed a finger at the map. 'There. It's got a vent in the back garden and it's also got a manhole just outside in the street.'

'We could get into the sewers there,' said the Health Inspector. 'How do these damn networks connect?' he said to Palmer.

The cockney ran his index finger over three or four of the sewer pipes which were shown in black on the map. 'All the pipes converge into one central chamber. The manholes are the routes into those vaults. That's what the numbered circles are. Each one of those has got a big chamber underneath it. There's one every two or three streets.'

Brady stroked his chin thoughtfully for a second.

'Could we crawl through those pipes? Like we did under that old woman's house?' he asked.

'We could, but we'd need special breathing apparatus. Those sewers are deeper than the rest. The pressure is far greater,' Palmer explained.

'What sort of apparatus is it?' Foley wanted to know.

'Just a face mask connected to an oxygen tank,' Palmer told him. 'But there's one snag. The tanks only hold enough air for thirty minutes.'

Another heavy silence descended finally broken by Brady.

'It's the only way. We have to go into the sewers.'

'What exactly do you think you can do?' Palmer demanded. 'If there's as many of those bloody things down there as you reckon, how the hell are you going to kill them all?'

'I'll crawl along the pipes,' said Brady, quietly.

Palmer shook his head. 'You'd never make it on your own. It's like a bloody maze down there.' He swallowed hard. 'I'll have to go down with you.'

The two men looked at each other for long moments then Brady continued.

'There's only one way of doing it,' he said. 'We'll have to crawl through the pipes and lure the slugs towards one of these central chambers. Once we've done that, you,' he looked at Foley, 'release the poison into the sewer.'

'You're acting as human bait,' said the curator, flatly.

'There's no other way,' Brady said.

'How the hell do I know where you are? Once you're down there, I won't be able to tell whereabouts in the pipes you are. If I release the poison while you're still down there, you'll be blown to pieces along with the slugs,' Foley said.

'We can keep in contact with two-way radios,' said Palmer. 'We use them all the time when we're working down there.'

Foley nodded.

'If we keep in constant contact, you can track us on the maps,' Palmer said.

'That's it then,' said Brady, flatly. 'Palmer and I will go into the sewers near Ron Bell's house. Foley, you track us on the two-way. We'll try and lead the slugs to one of the central chambers. Once we're there, give us five minutes to get out and then let the poison go.'

'And what if you're not out in time?' said the curator.

Brady hesitated a second. 'Let it go anyway.' He turned to Palmer. 'You don't have to do this you know.'

The little cockney looked at him. 'Like I said, you'd have no chance down there on your own. I can't stand by and let you kill yourself.'

'Brady. Don't you think it might be an idea to search that old house first, before you two go into the sewers?' said Foley. 'I mean, some of the slugs could still be in there.'

The Health Inspector nodded. 'You might be right. We'll do that first.' He turned to Palmer. 'You go and get the gear from the van, you and I will travel in that. Foley you take the poison in your own car.'

'What are you going to do?' asked the curator, watching as Brady made for the door.

He turned. 'I've got to make a phone call.'

Foley went to fetch the poison, Palmer scuttled off to fetch the equipment they would need and Brady wandered down to the enquiries desk. He perched on the edge of the desk and pulled the phone towards him, trying to steady his shaking hand as he dialled. Outside, the sky was like a blanket of mottled black velvet, just the pinpricks of stars glinting on it. The trees outside the museum swayed gently in the cool breeze, the wind blowing through their leaves like some disembodied voice. Brady drummed impatiently on the desk as he waited for the received to be picked up and, when it finally was, he recognised a familiar voice.

'Hello.'

'Kim,' he said.

'Mike, where the hell are you?' She sounded distraught. 'I called your office twice but there was no answer. I was getting ready to call the police, I wondered if you'd had an accident or ...'

He cut her short. 'Listen to me, love. I'm at the museum.'

'What are you doing there?'

'Foley's found a way to kill the slugs,' he told her.

'Mike,' her voice had taken on a note of pleading.

'We've got a good idea where they are. I'm going down into the sewers with one of the men from the department.'

He heard the first unmistakable beginnings of a sob.

'Mike, please don't. You'll...' Her voice was cracking.

'Kim. Listen to me. They've got to be destroyed.'

There was silence at the other end of the line, only the low crackle of static breaking the solitude.

'Kim,' he repeated.

'Yes.' Her voice was strained.

'I want you to keep all the taps covered and lock the doors and windows.'

Silence.

'Kim. Did you hear me?'

'Yes.'

He sucked in a tortured breath, wanting so much to be close to her, to hold her. 'I love you, Kim,' he said, swallowing hard.

She was quiet for a moment then he heard her thin, worried tones once more. 'You know, I was just thinking,' she said, laughing hollowly. 'How ridiculous it is for a man of forty to be crawling about in sewer pipes.' She was crying again, sobs jerking her body as she tried to retain her composure.

Brady gritted his teeth. 'I'm still thirty-nine,' he said, trying to laugh but it wouldn't come and he could only close his eyes as he listened to her crying.

'I love you,' she said, softly.

'Keep the supper warm eh?' he said, his voice sounding empty. He slowly replaced the receiver, sitting for a moment or two on the edge of the desk. He massaged the bridge of his nose between his thumb and forefinger and exhaled deeply. A moment later, Palmer appeared at the bottom of the stairs carrying an armful of things. He walked past Brady and up into the lab where he deposited the gear on a bench. The Health Inspector joined him.

'Put it on now, it'll save time,' said Palmer, thrusting a protective suit into the other man's hand. Both of them hurriedly pulled on the thick overalls, the little cockney completing the task first. He reached for one of the two-way radios which lay on the bench and handed it to Brady. 'Ever used one before?' he asked.

The Health Inspector shook his head and Palmer hastily demonstrated how the set worked, repeating the procedure when Foley joined them. The curator was pushing a metal drum before him and the other two men could hear fluid slapping about inside it.

'I'll need a hand to get it downstairs,' he said.

Brady helped the younger man with the bulky drum but, they eventually got it down the stairs and out into the waiting Volkswagen. The drum had a nozzle attachment to which Foley fitted a pipe. At the far end it sported what looked like the bowl of a watering can. He propped the large drum up on the passenger seat. Brady handed him the maps of the sewer and, after one final re-cap on the workings of the radio, he started the engine.

Palmer and Brady climbed into the white van and, with the breathing apparatus cradled on their laps, they drove off. Foley followed close behind.

Brady looked at his watch.

It was nearly ten fifteen p.m.

Less than fifteen minutes later, both vehicles pulled up outside Ron Bell's house.

Twenty-three

'There's the manhole cover,' said Palmer, pointing towards the large metal disc which lay in the road nearby.

Brady nodded. 'We'll look inside first.'

They clambered out of the van, leaving their masks and oxygen tanks on the seats. Foley was strolling across to join them. He'd pulled on a leather jacket just before they left but, despite the protection it offered, he was still shivering slightly.

'Cold?' said Brady.

Foley smiled, thinly. 'I'm not sure.'

'Come on,' said the Health Inspector and, led by him, they made their way up the path towards the front door of the house where Ron Bell had died. It looked even more forbidding in the darkness and Brady's mind was suddenly wrenched back to that hot morning weeks before when he and Archie Reece had discovered the mutilated remains. Weeks. It seemed like years since all this trouble began. Brady flicked on his torch and the powerful beam lanced through the darkness, lighting their way. He shone it over the front of the building and it reflected back off the dust covered windows. The waist high grass waved silently in the breeze and Foley cursed as he stepped into a patch of stinging nettles. The other two men looked round at him and he shrugged.

'We can get in along here,' said Brady, leading them towards the window which he and Reece had climbed through, what seemed like an eternity ago. Brady clambered through first, his nostrils immediately assailed by the stench of damp and decay. Next came Foley and, finally, Palmer who, as he was clambering in, accidentally brushed against a sliver of glass which opened a minute slit in his overalls at the top of the thigh.

The three men stood in what had once been the dining room and shone their torches around. The walls were peeling and the paint had come away to reveal layers of different colour, now faded and mildewed. The floorboards felt spongy as the men walked across them and Foley put a hand across his mouth, finding it difficult to breathe in the fetid atmosphere.

Something came hurtling at them from the shadows and Brady cursed.

It was a moth. It fluttered around for a second before disappearing through the broken window.

The trio moved on, into the sitting room where the corpse of Ron Bell had first been discovered. Brady showed them where the body had been lying. The room was completely empty. All the furniture had been removed, dust several inches thick showing where the sideboard had once stood. There were marks scored in the muck, tracing the path where the heavier objects had been dragged from the house. Their footsteps were strangely muffled as they moved about in the sitting room and the silence seemed to wrap itself around them like a cloak. Torch beams cut through the blackness, the tiny spots of light seeking clues, wondering if they were going to see the first slithering dark shape dragging itself along .

There were two doors leading out of the sitting room. One into the kitchen, the other into the hall.

'You two look upstairs,' said Brady. 'I'll check in there.' He moved towards the kitchen door while the other two men made their way out into the hall.

'If you find anything, shout,' Brady called after them.

'Don't worry,' Palmer said. 'If I see one of those bloody things, you'll be the first to know.'

Brady wandered into the kitchen, stopping for a second to listen to the heavy footfalls of his companions as they moved around upstairs. He could hear them going from room to room, the low murmur of their voices occasionally drifting through to him. Eventually, he turned his attention back to the kitchen, shining his torch across the filth-encrusted lino on the floor and across to the cupboards which had been ripped out long ago.

A spider had caught a crane-fly in its web and was busily devouring it. Brady held his torch on it for a second, watching the grisly tableau, then he moved the beam across towards another door to his right. As he walked towards it, Brady glanced out of the grime-encrusted windows of the kitchen and spied the sodium glare of the lamps which marked the first street on the new estate. He returned his attention to the other door, shining the torch onto the lock. There was no key and, optimistically, he turned the handle. Needless to say it didn't budge. The door was locked. He murmured something to himself and stepped back, the torch beam still directed at the peeling door. It was as he took that pace backward he noticed the small gap in the bottom of the door. He knelt to examine it, guessing it to be about two inches high. In one corner of the door something else caught his eye.

It was a slime trail.

It glistened in the torch light and Brady extended a gloved hand, touching the mucoid path with his index finger.

It was fresh.

He swallowed hard and stood up, trying the door once again, pushing his shoulder against it when it wouldn't open. But, the hinges were old and rusted and the Health Inspector heard them shriek in protest as he threw his weight against the door once again. This time the very wood itself seemed to crack. He stepped back and aimed a kick at the stubborn lock. The handle fell away, landing with a hollow thump on the lino.

'Nothing up there.'

The voice startled him and he spun round to see Foley and Palmer standing in the doorway.

'What have you found?' asked Foley.

Brady motioned to the door. 'It's a cellar or something.' He shone his torch down at the floor and both men saw the slime trail.

Palmer crossed to the door and both of them threw their weight against it, hearing the wood groan under the pressure. Finally, under their combined assault, it gave. It flew back on its hinges and slammed into the wall behind with a loud crash. The two men paused at the opening, gazing down into the blackness below. Brady swung his torch round but the beam would only penetrate the darkness a short distance. The stone steps of the cellar stretched away beneath them, the bottom invisible in the pitch black. A rancid stench rose from the cellar, an odour so rank it caused Brady to cough. He covered his nose with one hand and took a tentative step down. The torch beam wavered in his grasp and he had difficulty keeping his feet on the slippery steps. Step by step, he descended.

Palmer followed at an arm's length behind, using his own powerful torch to sweep the walls which crowded in on both sides of the staircase.

There were slime trails on them.

'Be careful,' he said, softly.

Brady could feel his heart thumping against his ribs as he neared the bottom of the steps. A thin film of perspiration had formed on his forehead. He directed the torch beam downwards, careful not to slip on the treacherous surface.

Two steps from the bottom he saw the first slug.

He stepped back, almost knocking Palmer over. The sewage man followed Brady's pointing finger and caught sight of the glistening black horror on the step, its posterior tentacles waving about soundlessly.

'What is it?' Foley called from the doorway.

'They're down here,' said Palmer, shining his torch over the floor of the cellar. The entire surface, every square inch of earth seemed to be covered by the slithering creatures. Like a glistening, undulating black carpet.

'I'll get the poison,' said Foley.

'No, wait,' Brady called and took a step down. He crushed the first slug beneath his heavy boot and walked on. He shone the torch over the slimy sea once more, noting that there were perhaps just two or three hundred of the creatures down there. Those closest were moving towards him but the Health Inspector merely backed off.

'What are you waiting for?' asked Palmer.

'We can't afford to waste any of that poison,' Brady told him. 'There aren't many of them here. That means that most must be in the sewer itself.'

'So, what do we do?' the sewer man wanted to know.

Brady put out a hand and felt the damp walls. 'You've got a can of petrol in the back of your van haven't you?'

Palmer nodded.

'Go and get it.'

The little cockney hesitated for a moment then hurried back up the stairs, past a bewildered Foley who was descending the steps.

'What the hell are you playing at, Brady?' he demanded, seeing the slugs slithering towards them. 'We've got to destroy them.'

'This isn't the nest,' said Brady. 'Look.' He shone the torch over the hundreds of slugs. 'The rest of them, the big ones, they *must* be down in the sewers.'

Palmer returned a moment later, the petrol can in his hand. Brady took it from him and unscrewed the cap then, watched by the other two men, he walked into the cellar dousing the carpet of writhing slugs in the reeking liquid. They tried to crawl up his legs but there weren't enough of them and Brady crushed many beneath his heavy boots. He made sure every last drop of the golden fluid was drained from the can then he threw it into the cellar and retreated back up the stairs to join his companions.

Foley handed him a box of matches and the Health Inspector struck one, its yellow glow illuminating his face briefly before he tossed it down into the black mass.

There was a high pitched 'whump' as the petrol went up, followed, a moment later by a series of pops and dull bangs as the flames destroyed the bodies of the slugs. Yellow flames danced in the blackness, devouring the hideous creatures and filling the cellar with choking black smoke.

'What about the house?' asked Palmer, watching the fire.

'It's so bloody damp in there the fire will burn itself out,' said Brady with some authority.

The three men watched for a moment longer then closed the cellar door behind them. They made their way hurriedly through the house, clambering back through the broken window.

As they passed the cellar bulkhead, a thin stream of smoke rose into the night air and they could still hear the pop and crackle as the slugs were incinerated.

Palmer looked back.

'Two hundred down, 20,000 to go,' he said cryptically.

Brady shot him an acid glance and the trio made their way out into the street. By the time they reached their parked vehicles, the smoke from the bulkhead was just a tiny plume of grey against the blackness of the night. Brady looked at it with something akin to satisfaction.

Palmer handed him his set of breathing apparatus and helped him to put it on, ensuring that he could breathe properly then the little man put on his own mask and tank. Their voices sounded muffled through the perspex and their breathing was heavy and laboured. Each of them picked up a two-way radio and Foley retrieved the third. Then, the three of them walked over to the curator's car where he quickly pulled the maps from the glove compartment.

'We're here,' Palmer told him, jabbing a gloved finger at the circle on the map marked sixteen.

Foley nodded. He got into his car and started the engine.

'We'd better synchronise watches,' said Brady.

They checked their time pieces.

'Keep in contact all the time,' said Foley and both men waved an acknowledgement.

'Remember,' said Brady. 'Five minutes after we give you the signal, let the poison go.'

The naturalist nodded and watched them as they strode over towards the manhole cover a few yards away.

It took both of them to move the huge metal disc, weighing, as it did, over a hundredweight. It fell to the road with a loud clang, spinning round and round like a dropped coin. Brady looked across at Palmer who tapped the cylinder of oxygen.

'Thirty minutes,' he said.

Brady nodded, noticing that the sewage man had a screwdriver stuck in his belt.

'What's that for?' he asked, pointing at it.

'Some of the pipes have grilles across them. I don't fancy getting caught in a dead end.'

Brady could feel his heartbeat quicken and he tried to control his breathing but it was difficult.

Led by Palmer, they began to descend.

It was eleven thirty p.m.

Twenty-four

Brady eased himself gently down from the metal ladder and stood beside Palmer, the effluent dribbling past them at about calf height. The Health Inspector swept the tunnel with his torch, noting that the beam was unable to penetrate the blackness for more than a few feet. Once again he felt that terrible claustrophobic feeling come over him as the walls of the pipe seemed to close in on him.

'We'd better check these out,' said Palmer, tapping the two-way. He switched his on and spoke into it.

Up above, the sudden crackle of static made Foley jump but the young curator picked up the set and held it to his ear.

'Foley, can you hear this?' asked Palmer, his voice buried beneath a crackling blanket of interference.

'Your voice is breaking up,' Foley told him, fiddling with the controls of the radio.

'Adjust the squelch button,' Palmer told him and, through the hissing static, Foley heard; 'Mary had a little lamb its fleece was brown not white...'

'Better,' said the naturalist.

Palmer continued, '...because the silly animal had rolled in its own shite.'

Foley laughed. 'OK, I've got it now.'

'Where the hell did you learn that?' asked Brady, smiling thinly.

Palmer shrugged and indicated that Brady should test his own equipment. A similar procedure was completed, then both men clipped the two-ways to their belts and bent low, ready to begin the tortuous crawl along the stretch of pipe which would lead to the first of the large central chambers. It was hot inside the suit and Brady felt even more uncomfortable with the breathing apparatus on. Although it was light, the tank of oxygen on his back seemed to weigh him down as he crawled and he could only hear the loud, guttural sound of his breathing as he struggled along behind Palmer. Every now and then the Health Inspector would stop, almost sitting in the flowing effluent, and shine his torch behind them, just to check that there were no slugs near them. He scanned the walls and roof of the pipe for slime trails but, as yet, saw none.

The meagre shaft of light which poured down the open manhole opening began to fade into darkness as they crawled deeper into the pipes. Brady scrambled on, anxious not to lose sight of Palmer who was about two feet ahead of him.

They passed a side outlet which was less than a foot in diameter and both men concentrated their torches into the black hole.

'Drain outlet,' Palmer told him.

Satisfied that nothing was moving in there, the two men crawled on, now totally surrounded by the cloying darkness. It seemed to swathe itself around them like a shroud and the Health Inspector felt the first drops of perspiration forming on his face. His breathing was heavy and, for a second, he wondered if he might use up his oxygen supply too quickly. The vision of Kim swam into his mind and he tried to push it to one side. Her joke about a forty-year-old man crawling around sewers was beginning to take on extra significance. He closed his eyes tight, until white stars danced before him and the vision of her finally left him. He continued crawling, the progress surprisingly fast, his torch constantly sweeping the pipe in its search for the first tell-tale signs of the slugs.

Palmer stopped.

Brady shone his torch past the little cockney and saw that a grille barred their way. The sewage man pulled the screwdriver from his belt and began working on the first of the rusty rivets which held the grille in place. Brady crouched beside him and pulled the two-way from his own belt.

'Foley,' he said. 'We've reached a grille. We should be through it in a couple of minutes.'

183

Foley acknowledged and traced their progress on the map before him.

'Another thirty feet and you'll be at the first chamber,' the younger man told him. 'Any sign of the slugs yet?'

'Nothing moving down here except us,' Brady told him.

He clipped the radio back into place and watched as Palmer prized the last rusty screw loose. He stuck the heavy screwdriver into the jaws of the grille and put all his weight on it. The grid came free and the little man tossed it away. It landed with a clang behind them. Some rotted faeces slopped onto Brady's overalls and he paled, fighting back the nausea. He shone the torch behind them once more then waited as Palmer crawled through to take the lead again.

Up above, Foley started the engine of the Volkswagen and drove slowly to the next red circle on the map, the site of the next manhole and the central chamber. He parked the car on one side of the road and guessed that it would take them about five minutes to crawl as far as the next vault. The young man exhaled deeply. He hoped that the chamber wouldn't become their crypt. A quick glance at his watch told him that they had less than twenty-five minutes.

It was eleven forty p.m.

Brady and Palmer continued on their journey, passing two more outlets as they did so. They were much larger than the first one they'd encountered and the men found that their torch beams could not penetrate the darkness in those particular pipes.

'It's a connecting pipe from one of the other main flow pipes,' said Palmer, peering into the first of the outlets.

He could see nothing in the darkness and he swallowed hard, even shining his torch into the river of effluent which occasionally washed up as high as his elbows. He, too, was beginning to perspire and he knew that it wasn't because of the suit. All he could think of was that he hadn't got the chance to kiss his kids goodnight. The little devils were probably still up, waiting for him to get home. His wife would wonder what he was up to as well. He could imagine her moaning about how his dinner would be spoiled but, at that precise moment in time, Palmer would have given his right arm to have heard her nagging. To be up on the surface, at home. Instead of fifty feet below the ground acting as live bait for thousands of man-eating slugs.

The river of effluent did not flow high enough to alert him to the rip in his overalls.

He turned back from the outlet and looked at Brady who had been checking the other hole.

'Can't see a bloody thing,' he said.

'Me neither,' Brady told him.

They moved on.

It was a moment or two before the first of the slugs emerged from the larger of the outlets. Moving effortlessly in the slimy environment, it slithered over the damp wall of the pipe, the scent of man reaching it despite the assortment of smells down there.

In a matter of seconds, the entire pipe was filling with the obscene black monstrosities and, across from the first group, more were spilling from the second outlet. They slid into the water, others crawled along the roof and walls of the pipe, keeping just out of range of the probing torch beams. It was almost as if they knew.

Brady and Palmer crawled on unaware that, less than ten feet behind, the seething black mass of slugs pursued them.

The two men reached the first of the central chambers and Brady was glad to find that he could stand up for a minute. He shone his torch around, noting that the vault was about twelve feet in diameter. A rough circle with half a dozen outlets flowing into it. The effluent river was flowing swiftly here and it gushed past their feet with a low hiss. He shone his torch up and saw the iron ladder which led up to the manhole. Both of them knew that Foley was up there. Waiting.

'Which pipe do we go into next?' asked the Health Inspector, shining his torch over the numerous black holes. They seemed to yawn open like huge mouths, screaming a silent warning to the men.

Palmer took the radio from his belt and raised it to his masked face.

'Foley,' he said. 'We're in the first chamber. On that map, there should be one outlet pipe marked in red, which one is it?'

Up in the car, the curator scanned the black and red lines, his finger quivering slightly as he finally found what he was looking for.

'There's about half a dozen outlets,' he said, vaguely.

'I know that,' snapped Palmer. 'Which one is marked in red?'

Foley found it. 'If you're standing with your backs to the main pipe then it's the one second from the left.'

Palmer clipped the radio back onto his belt and led Brady towards the designated outlet. They were forced to crawl once more as they entered it and the Health Inspector felt the muscles in his arms and back beginning to ache as he dragged himself along. They made their way slowly through the next pipe which seemed to narrow the deeper they got into it, but Brady told himself that his imagination was beginning to get the better of him and he struggled on behind Palmer.

He stopped suddenly as he heard a splashing from behind them.

He stuck out a hand to halt Palmer's progress.

'Listen,' said Brady and both men held their breath, torches directed down the pipe along which they had just crept. The powerful beams showed nothing.

'What was it?' asked Palmer.

Brady waved a hand to silence the sewage man and then the cockney himself heard it - the loud splashing which seemed to be growing nearer.

'It's probably just the water flowing into the chamber,' he said, reassuring no one, including himself. 'We'd better move on.'

He started to crawl again but Brady remained still, his ears and eyes alert for the slightest sound or movement. He kept the torch beam directed behind him for long moments before finally crawling along behind Palmer. Perhaps the sewage man had been right. Perhaps it had just been the water gushing into the chamber.

Behind them, the vault was filled to overflowing with the black creatures, all slipping and sliding over one another in their haste to reach the two humans just three or four yards ahead.

'We should be reaching another of the chambers soon,' said Palmer, his own breath coming in gasps. His knees ached from crawling so much and he paused for a second beside a connecting pipe to get his breath.

Brady crouched beside him and rolled up the sleeve of his overall. He shone the torch onto his watch.

'Eleven forty-five,' he said. 'Fifteen minutes of air left.'

Palmer nodded. The Health Inspector patted him on the shoulder and they prepared to move on but, before they did, he swept the tunnel once more with his torch light.

There, glistening on the roof of the pipe, were a dozen slime trails.

'Palmer, look,' said Brady, pointing to the mucoid paths.

The sewage man turned his attention to the slime, watching as the Health Inspector touched it with a gloved finger. As he pulled it away, gobs of transparent fluid dripped from the material.

The trails were fresh.

The two men followed their course to a small outlet which Palmer said fed in from a drain. Brady bent close and shone his torch inside.

'My God,' he murmured and Palmer directed the beam of his own light inside.

Half a dozen of the slugs were in there, most of them larger than six inches. For long seconds they seemed to recoil from the bright lights but then, slowly, they began slithering towards the two men.

'Let's move,' said Brady and they suddenly found renewed strength, scrambling quickly down the pipe towards what they knew to be the second chamber.

Brady shone the torch behind him, puzzled when he saw no sign of the slugs.

There was a sibilant hiss which made both men gasp and it was a second or two before they realized that it was the static on the radio.

Foley was trying to contact them.

Brady snatched his two-way angrily from his belt.

'What is it?' he snapped. 'You scared the shit out of us.'

Palmer looked across at him. 'No pun intended I hope,' he grinned.

'Have you seen anything?' the curator wanted to know.

'We've seen half a dozen of them,' Brady told him.

'They're down here all right, it's just a matter of where.'

'Is it working?'

'If you mean are they following us, I don't know.'

Palmer tapped him on the shoulder.

'We'd better move on,' he said.

Brady nodded and switched off the set again, clipping it to his belt.

The two men found that the pipe curved slightly, eventually branching out into a kind of fork, presenting them with a choice of which one to enter. Palmer was about to radio through for directions when he saw the first of the slugs spilling from the left hand pipe ahead of them.

'Oh Jesus,' he said and tugged at Brady's arm.

The Health Inspector snatched for his radio.

'Foley,' he shouted into the set. 'We've found them.'

'Where are you?' the curator wanted to know.

It was Palmer who spoke next. 'They've got in front of us. They must have come from the second chamber. We'll have to go back the way we came.'

With the slugs less than a yard behind, the two men twisted awkwardly in the narrow pipe and scrambled back towards the first huge chamber. Brady now leading, held his torch before him and he was the first to see the other group of slugs. Those that had been pursuing them now blocked their way to the first chamber.

The two men were pinned between different groups of the black monstrosities, their route to the first and second chambers blocked off.

The seething mass approached slowly from both sides.

'In there,' shouted Palmer, pushing Brady towards a narrow outlet. 'It's a connecting pipe, it should take us through to another flow pipe.'

Brady squeezed through the narrow tunnel, finding it so confined that he had to crawl on his stomach to get through. His oxygen tank scraped against the stonework and the effluent splashed up against the perspex of his face mask but he crawled on, using his knees and elbows as means of propulsion. He slithered along - like the monstrosities which pursued him.

Palmer threw himself into the narrow opening behind the Health Inspector, pushing the older man along in an effort to escape the hungry black hordes.

'Foley,' shouted the sewage man into his radio. 'They've got us trapped. We're in a connecting pipe mid-way between the first and second chambers. Where will we end up if we keep crawling?'

The curator's voice sounded a million miles away as he spoke.

'You should come into another flow pipe, if you crawl down that it'll bring you back out into the first chamber again,' he told them, tracing their progress on the map. His own heart was now thumping madly against his ribs. He started the engine of the Volkswagen again and drove to the centre of the road. There, he pushed open the passenger door and struggled to lift the heavy drum of poison onto the tarmac. With perspiration running from his face, he managed to push it over towards the manhole cover. Then, he bent and took a hold of the metal bar across the top of the heavy iron disc.

It wouldn't budge an inch.

The sewer remained sealed.

Brady was crawling as fast as he could through the rancid effluent, his breath coming in gasps. Behind him, Palmer was able to see the slugs as the first of them slithered into the pipe and made for his heavy boots. He crushed the first half a dozen beneath the weighty footwear but, in the beam of his torch, he could see more and more of the black things swarming into the tunnel. Fear gripped him tightly, and he found it difficult to swallow.

'Move,' he shouted to Brady.

The Health Inspector was scrambling along as fast as his aching limbs would allow but, suddenly, he let out a mournful groan.

The other end of the pipe was blocked by a grille.

'Give me the screwdriver, quick,' he bellowed, looking back to see the tunnel filling with the obscene fat slugs, all eager to reach their prey.

Palmer tore the implement from his belt and handed it to Brady who didn't even bother trying to loosen the screws, he merely jammed the blade between the slats and tried to tear the grid free. The screws were rusty, the stonework decaying, but still the recalcitrant grille kept its place, barring their escape.

'Hurry,' screamed Palmer, the leading slugs now seething over his legs, trying to bite through the thick material of his protective suit.

Brady beat at the grille with his hands in an effort to loosen it and, finally, the metal started to give. One screw came away and the Health Inspector used all his strength on the screwdriver, using the implement like a lever to tear off the grid.

'For fuck's sake,' shrieked Palmer and then he screamed in agony as the first slug found the rent in his suit and began eating its way into his thigh.

'Brady,' Palmer screamed but the Health Inspector could do nothing to help him. He just continued to wrench at the stubborn grille, hearing his companion's shrieks of pain. In that confined space they seemed to be deafening and Brady wanted to scream himself.

Blood spurted up from the gash in Palmer's leg and he tore at the first slug, managing to rip its vile form from his leg. But its head remained embedded in the flesh and it was just the bloated body which he tossed away. And now more of the creatures were swarming over him, tasting the fast-flowing blood, burrowing deep into his meaty thigh, sliding up inside the suit until they reached his genitals. The sewer man shrieked again as two of the slugs began boring their way into his scrotum. He felt waves of unbelievable pain lance through him as more of the creatures found the rip in the suit. They slithered inside to feast on his shaking body. He tried to swat at them with his hands, feeling one huge fat body burst under his fist. It squashed against his torn thigh, its own pus-like bodily fluid mingling with his spurting blood.

Brady began to shout in rage and terrified frustration when the grille wouldn't come away and, behind him, Palmer's screams became fainter as the slugs ate their way into him, a number burrowing up through his torn genitals, using his anus as a means of access in their search for the softer, more succulent parts of his body. Blood filled his mouth and gushed out into his face mask, bubbling up behind the perspex, running back down the tube to the oxygen cylinder until he was breathing the coppery fumes of his own life fluid.

With an angry yell, Brady finally tore the grid free.

He slithered through and found himself, as Foley had said, in another flow-pipe.

He shot out a hand and began to haul Palmer free of the connecting tunnel but it was too late, the little man was already dead. The only movements his body made were spasmodic contractions of the muscles and now many of the slugs were sliding over his torn body in their efforts to reach Brady.

Panting for air, the Health Inspector began to crawl back towards the first chamber.

He had just five minutes of oxygen left.

Foley tried one last time to remove the manhole cover but could make no impression on the heavy disc. Looking around in panic he saw a piece of wood lying by the roadside - the branch of a tree torn down by some kids a day before. He hurried across to it, relieved to find that it was reasonably stout. The curator stuck it into the indentation in the lid and put all his weight on it.

The lid still refused to move and Foley put more pressure on it.

There was a loud groan and the wood snapped.

He threw one half to the ground, his mind desperately searching for a means to lift the heavy lid.

The radio crackled and he snatched it up.

'Yes,' he said.

'Foley.' The curator recognised Brady's voice. 'The slugs are right behind me,' he gasped. 'I'm coming up. Get ready to let the poison in.'

Foley hesitated a second. 'I can't get the lid up,' he said, flatly.

'Oh God. Have you tried prizing it open?' gasped the Health Inspector .

Foley said that he had.

'For Christ's sake, hurry,' Brady implored him. 'I'm at the main chamber now, the bloody things are right behind me.' His voice rose to a shout. 'Hurry, Foley.'

'Rope,' the naturalist said aloud and hurried to the boot of his car. He flung it open and rummaged through the other debris in search of the thick hemp which he knew to be in there.

He found it and scurried back to the manhole cover where he slipped the rope under the metal bar in the lid. He tied a hasty knot, tugged on the rope then secured the other end to his front bumper. Then he leapt behind the wheel and reversed slowly.

Inch by agonising inch, the lid began to lift.

Foley smiled, triumphantly.

It was almost halfway up when the rope began to fray.

Brady stood in the central chamber looking up, watching as the lid was lifted. He shot a glance towards the pipes which opened into the vault and shuddered.

From every outlet, hundreds of black shapes were spilling. Like an unstoppable tide of death, they poured out of the pipes into the central chamber and Brady could only guess at how many thousand there were. Led by the huge seven and eight inch monsters, they piled on top of one another, gliding effortlessly towards their helpless prey.

He stood transfixed for long seconds, watching as the seething black mass drew towards him, then, he grabbed at the metal ladder and began to climb towards the rapidly opening gap above him.

The slugs reached the spot where he had been standing and he saw a number trying to slither up the ladder after him but they could gain no adequate hold and fell back amongst the rest of their companions.

Brady was halfway up the ladder now and his oxygen was running out rapidly. His head felt swollen, as if someone were filling it with air. The ladder swam before him and, once, he nearly lost his footing but he continued up, gripping each rung tighter than the next until he was mere feet from the opening.

It was at that point that the rope snapped.

All Foley heard was the dull clang as the manhole cover fell back into place. He looked round in alarm and saw what had happened, leaping from behind the steering wheel to re-affix the rope. He could hear Brady's weak banging on the bottom of the lid as he fastened the hemp once more. Then the Health Inspector's voice drifted wearily over the two-way.

'Running out of oxygen,' he groaned. 'I can't breathe. I...'

Brady found himself nearing unconsciousness, he looked down into the darkness and saw the slugs seething about below him almost as if they were waiting for him to drop into their midst. He lost his footing and thought he was going to faint but he gritted his teeth, trying to hold his breath to prevent himself inhaling his own carbon dioxide. He heard the roar of the Volkswagen's engine and then suddenly, the manhole cover was torn free. In a daze, Brady felt strong arms grabbing him, pulling him from that hell hole. He felt hands struggling to remove his mask and then he was breathing fresh air again. Fresh clean air.

His head was throbbing but he scrambled to his feet when he saw Foley struggling with the large drum of poison, attempting to tip it over.

Brady joined him and both men put their weight to it, feeling the drum teeter then finally fall.

Five gallons of the deadly substance spilled from it and rained down into the sewer, onto the writhing slugs.

There was a flash of light so brilliant that both men thought they must be blinded, then a blistering geyser of white flame rose almost silently from the manhole. It rocketed up into the heavens a full fifty feet before disappearing in a billowing mushroom cloud of grey smoke. The ground shook as, beneath them, the poison set off a chain reaction which swept through the. entire sewer system of Merton. As Palmer had warned them, the fire-flash set off the clouds of methane and the earth rocked. Both Foley and Brady were thrown to the floor and, below a lightning tongue of flame tore along the pipes in all directions, fanning out like some kind of fiery amoebic creature. Tentacles of screaming flame ripped through pipes and tunnels. The taps in the houses nearby were blasted from their housings and in many places, the water boiled in lavatory bowls. In the street nearby, a manhole cover was blasted a full thirty feet into the air by the explosion and, all over town, sewer vents lit up momentarily as the flames roared beneath them.

Then, as suddenly as it had come, the fire died and just a mournful plume of grey smoke wafted up from the open hole.

Brady rose slowly to his feet, the smell of burning strong in his nostrils. A moment later Foley joined him and both of them peered down into the smoke-filled maw below. They could see nothing.

'I'm sorry about Palmer,' said Foley, softly.

The Health Inspector nodded. 'The slugs killed him. The poor bastard was dead before the explosion.'

Brady was suddenly aware of a foul smell and he realized that it was his overalls. Pieces of dried excrement still stuck to them in places and he hurriedly pulled them off, dropping the stinking garments in an untidy heap on the road beside the manhole.

'What now?' asked Foley.

The Health Inspector exhaled deeply. 'The sewers will have to be checked. We can't take any chances. I'll go down again in the morning with some more men, just to be sure.'

It was as they turned to head back to Foley's car that they saw it.

Crawling in the road was a single solitary slug.

'Oh my God,' whispered Brady.

Before he could react, Foley had snatched up one of the discarded gloves and was moving towards the slug which looked to be about two or three inches long. He knelt and, watched by Brady, picked the black creature up. It tried to contract itself, anxious to be free of the grip and, when Brady stepped closer he saw that the animal had retracted its posterior tentacles.

Foley put it down on the pavement and it crawled away towards the safety of the bushes nearby.

Brady breathed an audible sigh of relief.

'Looks like my theory was right,' said Foley but there was no joy in his words, just a thankful affirmation of his beliefs. 'Let's wait and see shall we,' said Brady, patting the younger man on the back.

Lights were going on in houses all over the street, people were peering out of doors and windows and, far away, the two men heard the wail of police and ambulance sirens.

'I think you and I are going to have some questions to answer,' said Foley, pulling a packet of cigarettes from his pocket.

Brady nodded. 'Don Palmer's wife will have to be told,' he said, softly.

'The police will do it,' said Foley.

'No. It was my fault he died. It's my job to tell her.'

'He knew the risks involved,' said Foley.

'Yeah. But I'm still going to be the one to tell her.' Foley offered him a cigarette.

'I don't smoke,' Brady said.

'Perhaps it's time you started,' said the curator and both men smiled.

Epilogue

George Thomas watched as the crates of lettuce were unloaded from the back of the lorry. He chewed the end of his pipe which, as always, remained unlit.

All around him the place was alive with the sound of crashing boxes, raised voices, laughing. The usual cacophony of noise which went to make up Covent Garden.

He'd arrived later than usual that morning due to the traffic on the roads leading into London. The drive from his farm in Merton usually took him less than an hour but he'd left at five a.m. that morning, when the mist still lay heavy on the ground, and now at seven o'clock he had finally managed to struggle through. The sun was already high in the sky above the city, pouring its unrelenting heat down over the people scurrying for buses and tubes.

George always hated coming to London. He'd lived in the country all his life and the hustle and bustle of the city unsettled him. Everybody was always in such a bloody hurry and George liked to take things easy. However, at sixty-two he was as sprightly as a teenager and ran his little farm in Merton only with the help of his two sons. It was a small piece of land but it yielded a good crop of vegetables and George had found a regular buyer for his produce. He watched now as the man picked quickly but expertly through the crates laid out before him, occasionally taking out one of the lettuces and tossing it onto a nearby pile of rotting vegetables. He went along all the crates with similar expertise, muttering to himself as he did.

'Good crop again,' said George.

'Yeah, only a few bad ones,' said the buyer, picking up another lettuce. He ran an expert eye over it, noticing something inside the inner leaves. He threw it onto the pile with the other rejects.

After about fifteen minutes he finished. The deal was concluded and George climbed thankfully back into his lorry. He waved a hurried farewell to his buyer, who was already having the crates removed, and then set off to battle his way through the traffic on his way home to Merton.

He couldn't wait to be out of the bloody city.

The pile of discarded vegetables grew higher as the day progressed, until it seemed to tower as tall as a man. Under the heat of the sun the green stuff began to wilt and smell, but no one paid it any attention. People came and went and the noise grew louder, with stall-holders shouting out their prices, bickering with their neighbours. It was a normal day really.

No one paid the slightest attention to the lettuce which lay near the bottom of the pile, one of George's crop, rejected because of the strange cylindrical objects in its inner leaves. The transparent mucoid tubes with the black centres.

Who cared about a few slugs' eggs anyway?